Beyond the Keeper's Gate

Fred,
Pursue God!
Enjoy!
Lauren Warner

Beyond the Keeper's Gate

Ladean Warner

Mélange press
Round Lake, NY

Published by
Mélange Press
a division of Word Alchemy, Inc.
5 Albany Avenue
PO Box 696
Round Lake, NY 12151

Library of Congress Control Number: 2010926960

ISBN 978-0-9824337-7-5

Printed in the United States of America

Book design by Kimberley Debus
Cover design by Cindy Hermann
Cover Photography by Jami LaCasse

Dedicated to my husband and best friend, Joe,
for believing in me and loving me.
I'm truly blessed to have you in my life!

PROLOGUE

In a Dublin cemetery, a lone mourner stood under a burlap canopy that was whipping in the wind offering little shelter from the pelting rain. His thick white hair was matted to his head as he stood with his head bowed, listening to the old priest's homily. Robert Donovan was not related to the deceased, but he had been his attorney for over fifty years.

No family joined Donovan on the Irish hillside that held a few isolated graves. Hidden in the back of the graveyard, this small section held the bodies of a particular group of men. The original grave was occupied by the man who had purchased these plots and gated them back around 1850. It was at his request that in the following years, these men would join him in this place. He had a small sign engraved with "The Keeper's Gate" and hung it on the fence. Most refused the funeral ceremony, as had Donovan's client, but it was Donovan, seeking appeasement for his own guilt, who had requested the old priest perform the last rites for his client. Donovan doubted that God would give his client absolution for his sins, but it helped to ease his own conscience to have the ceremony performed. The secrets Donovan harbored he would later confess to the old priest in order to seek absolution for his own part in the heinous crimes his client had committed.

Even in death, the recently departed Shamus O'Leary had a hold on Donovan. Bobby Donovan had been a young new lawyer with no experience when he met O'Leary a half century ago. Untried as a lawyer, Donovan worked as a law clerk for his father hoping for a chance to prove himself. But one fateful day, O'Leary walked into the old law firm and found Bobby. Against his father's advice, Bobby was eager to accommodate his only client's wishes. Now, over fifty years later, Donovan's one client had made him rich, but now he wished that he had never met O'Leary.

When O'Leary had been arrested six years before, Donovan tried to get his client to confess to the numerous crimes he committed, but he had refused. O'Leary said that he still needed to protect the creature even though he had spent his final years in a Dublin prison. The papers in Ireland and England headlined the capture of The Keeper, giving rise again to the old myths and legends. But it quickly became old news.

Donovan shuffled his feet and looked up as the old priest, having said the final prayer, turned from the grave. A few workmen stood to the side with shovels waiting for Donovan to leave as well, but he just stood staring out at the rain. Donovan felt the weight of three envelopes in his coat pocket that he was required to mail as soon as he left. He had hoped that in death the work that O'Leary had done was over. But it wasn't. The three envelopes that would be headed for the United States would open old wounds and continue the evil. Donovan pleaded with O'Leary to end this, to let the evil die with him instead of allowing another to carry on looking after some mythical creatures. But the letters were written and held until this appointed day.

The workmen came to the grave and began the final burial tasks. Donovan stood watching until all the work was done. Finally, he stepped out from under the canopy and walked toward his car. The rain poured down from the heavens, soaking him through. The weight of guilt and foreboding caused him to stumble as he reached his car. Rain mingled with tears on his cheeks as he realized that he would have no choice but to mail the envelopes. Somehow Donovan knew the creature would know, and he would be punished if he failed.

CHAPTER 1

The August sun was hot as Meg Riley sat at an outdoor café on Broadway, the main drag in Saratoga Springs, New York. The sidewalks and streets were crowded with tourists. The heat didn't seem to stop people from strolling down the busy avenue or enjoying the outdoor cafés. Dressed in a white sundress with tiny green leaves and a wide-brimmed hat, Meg easily fit into the diverse Saratoga crowd. The leaves on her dress complemented her green eyes and shoulder length blonde hair. A private investigator, she wanted to blend in so that the man she was following wouldn't suspect he was being watched.

Two teen-aged boys walked down Broadway toward Congress Park. One of them was laughing at something his friend said as he glanced at the outdoor tables in front of them. He made eye contact with Meg, and there seemed to be a moment of recognition. She half-smiled at him, not really knowing who he was. It suddenly felt a lot hotter to her as they walked past her table. She turned to watch the boys. The one who seemed to recognize her looked back over his shoulder, and Meg realized she was still watching him.

Meg continued watching until the boys disappeared into the crowd. There was something about that kid that was familiar, but she couldn't place him. She turned her attention back to the man, who was inside the restaurant with his girlfriend. But the table was empty and a busboy was clearing it. She quickly scanned the crowd and saw a black sports car driving away with her couple in it.

Swearing under her breath, Meg picked up her handbag and dropped the tiny camera inside. Aside from a few pictures of them eating, Meg had nothing to prove to her client that her husband was cheating on her. Meg motioned to the waitress and pulled out some money. She handed the waitress the bills and then tucked the novel she was pretending to read in the crook of her arm. Meg walked down Broadway until she reached a doorway between two stores. She opened the door and stepped into the cool air conditioned stairwell that led to her second floor office.

At the top of the stairs, she unlocked a door and stepped into the reception area. It was lunchtime, so her assistant, Allison, was out. Meg was glad for the respite, since her failure at the café had unnerved and bothered her. She didn't want to explain anything to Allison right now. She went into her office and closed the door. Turning on her computer, she plugged the tiny camera into the USB port and began to download the pictures to her computer. She was disappointed in letting herself become distracted from her job.

Meg pulled her hat off and threw it onto the desk. She stood up and walked to the long windows next to her desk that faced Broadway. She looked down at the people on the street and thought about that boy again. Finally, she remembered who he was. Sam Craig. It had been six long years since she saw him last, but she would never forget him. He had changed so much since that little boy that Meg knew, but he was forever part of the case that made her famous and destroyed her police career.

Meg had been a detective on the Granelle Police force when Sam Craig disappeared twice. Meg had been working on the case that involved two missing local women when Sam ran away. The second time, she was sure he had run away when his mother had died in what looked like an accident. That was until Meg was abducted and woke up in a basement with Sam and the other missing women.

In working on the case, Meg had become a target for the madman who had thought he was the fulfillment of an old Irish myth. The clues that she found led her to the old myths about a keeper of some dark creatures, clues that her captain thought were a waste of time. When she continued to pursue her theory, Meg was suspended from the police force, but she didn't give up and soon found herself the victim of the madman, Trevor Grant. Even when the case was solved and the captain begrudgingly told her she was right, it was never the same between them. Meg's working conditions eroded because she refused to take orders from her boss.

In the midst of this discontentment, a woman named Andrea Schuman called Meg. She knew Meg had been the one who solved the case of the missing women and she was desperate to find a private investigator in Saratoga. Certain her husband was cheating on her, Mrs. Schuman offered Meg a small fortune to follow her husband and take pictures of his exploits. Not only did Meg get the pictures, but she made a great witness for Mrs. Schuman and her reputation as a detective ensured Mrs. Schuman a huge divorce settlement.

Soon Meg found that she had so much private investigative work that she resigned from the police department and opened her office in Saratoga. She was glad to leave Granelle, not only to distance herself from the force, but also from Jake Peterson. Once, Jake had been her partner on the police force and her fiancé, but that was before he turned religious and became a minister. Meg had been fine with just being his friend, but soon Jake met someone else. Even though it had been years since Meg and Jake had planned a future together, it hurt her so much to see him happy with another woman. After seeing so many couples cheating, lying, and hurting each other, Meg couldn't help but wonder if Jake was any different just because he was religious now.

The computer beeped as the camera finished downloading the pictures. Meg turned from the window, still wondering about Sam. The last she knew of Sam, he and his family had moved to Poughkeepsie to escape from the loss of his mother and the memories of Sam's abduction. She wondered what brought him back to Saratoga. Now that she had lost track of her latest client's husband, maybe she would take a walk down Broadway and see if she could find out what Sam was up to now.

Meg closed her door and changed into shorts and a T-shirt. The phone rang and she let it go to voicemail. She knew Allison would be back soon and would listen to the message. She picked up her handbag from where she had dropped it next to her desk, left the office, and locked the door.

Back on Broadway, Meg headed down the sidewalk toward Congress Park, following the path of the two boys. She glanced into stores as she walked, looking for them. Stopped by a traffic light across from the park, she looked up Congress Street, wondering which way to go. She shrugged and went down the sidewalk toward the plaza, where a laser-tag arcade was located, hoping the boys went to play.

An hour later, Meg was hot and tired from walking around Saratoga, so she went back to her office to find it was still locked. Frustrated, Meg unlocked the door and saw the light flashing on her phone. She listened to her messages, only to find that Allison had called over an hour ago to say she was sick and not coming back to work that afternoon. Well, the day was shot anyway. Meg decided she would take a drive out to Granelle and see if she could find out anything about Sam Craig from her old friend, Mo Reynolds.

CHAPTER 2

That night, Sarah Peterson stood on the back porch of her house, her immediate surroundings illuminated by the dim porch light. The darkness shrouded the back yard and the surrounding woods. Although her long black hair was pulled back in a ponytail and she was dressed in shorts and a tank top, she was uncomfortably hot while outside the comfort of her air conditioned house. Sarah could hear the sound of the wildlife that lived in the woods beyond her house, and she stood listening.

Sarah cupped her hands around her mouth and called out, "Felix, where are you? Come on in." Somewhere in the woods a bird screeched. She called out again, "Felix!" She squinted her deep brown eyes and tried to make out anything in the darkness. She thought she saw movement just within the woods.

"Felix, is that you?" Sarah called out again. Rushing toward her at breakneck speed came her black and white cat with all its hair standing on end. It reached the safety of her feet and crouched down, growling at something unseen in the woods. Sarah leaned down to pick him up, but he pawed at her hand, hissing. Felix looked back toward the woods and meowed from deep in his throat. Sarah had never seen her normally friendly cat act like this. She looked back to the woods and could see a dark shape rushing toward a tree in the yard. Red eyes glared from the darkness.

Gasping, Sarah turned quickly and opened the door. Felix almost tripped her as they both rushed inside. Sarah pulled the storm door closed behind her and looked back into the night. The dark shape seemed to be still near the tree, but Sarah couldn't tell for certain now that she was in the bright kitchen. She shut off the back porch light and the whole yard disappeared into shadows. She closed the inside door and turned the deadbolt. Laughing at herself, she realized that whatever that animal was, it couldn't open the door anyway. She turned to search for her frightened cat.

Sarah went to the cupboard and took out a bag of cat food. She shook the bag and called to Felix again. She never would have named the tuxedo cat

Felix, but he was a gift from her husband. He had dubbed the cat Felix because he said the feline looked just like the cartoon cat.

"Felix, aren't you hungry? Come here, kitty," Sarah called. She poured some food in a ceramic bowl on the floor in the kitchen. When he didn't come, Sarah went into the living room to find him. She found her husband's German shepherd curled up on the couch sleeping.

"Buddy," Sarah scolded. "Get off the couch." The big dog opened his eyes and stretched, but didn't move. "You know you're not supposed to be on the couch."

Sarah went to the couch and pushed Buddy until he relented and crawled off the couch. He went over to the big Oriental rug in front of the stone fireplace and plopped down again. Sarah stood with her hands on her hips watching him and then looked back at the couch. Dog hair covered the cushion that Buddy had been sleeping on. Her husband told her just to cover the couch with a sheet since Buddy had been in the habit of sleeping on the couch long before they got married, but Sarah insisted she could train Buddy to sleep on the floor. After three years, she was still pushing Buddy off, not only from the couch, but out of their bed.

With a deep sigh, Sarah went back to search for Felix. She finally found herself in her husband's office, the last place she thought Felix would be. Her husband was sitting at his desk, working on his computer.

"What's wrong?" he asked her.

"It's Felix," she said as she looked behind a love seat that was in the corner of the office. "Something outside scared him. Now I can't find him." She got on her hands and knees and looked under the furniture.

"What could have scared him?"

"I'm not sure, but I saw something that was just like a dark shadow. It came rushing out of the woods, and its eyes were glowing red. It even scared me a little." She stood up and looked around the room for a place the cat could have hidden.

"What did you just say?" he asked. The tone of his voice made her stop looking for Felix and look at him.

"Jake, what's wrong?" Jake's face had paled.

"What did you see?"

"I couldn't tell. Just a dark shadow, like a dog," Sarah said coming over to the desk. "What's wrong?"

"About the eyes. What did you say about the eyes?" Jake asked slowly, getting to his feet. At six feet tall, Jake hovered over his tiny wife. His deep blue eyes penetrated hers and concern was etched across his handsome face.

"All I could see were the eyes in the darkness because they were reflected by the porch light. Jake, you're starting to scare me. What's wrong?" Sarah reached out to him, and Jake pulled her close and hugged her.

"I didn't mean to scare you. But it sounds like that creature."

Sarah pulled away and looked up at his face. "What creature?" she asked.

"It was long before you came to Granelle." Jake paused. "Where was it? I want to see."

"In the backyard."

They walked to the kitchen and opened the back door. Sarah turned on the light and pointed to the tree where she saw the shadow. The moon had come up over the woods, and the backyard was washed in moonlight. Whatever had been in the yard was gone. Jake got a flashlight out of a drawer in the kitchen and went out anyway.

Nervously, Sarah picked up the cordless phone and stood on the porch, watching him. Jake looked behind the tree that Sarah pointed out and then at the edge of the woods. He looked deep into the woods, but didn't find anything. Sarah felt relieved when Jake finally came back toward the house. He turned one last time and flashed the light toward the woods.

They went back into the kitchen and Jake put the flashlight on the counter. "Don't let Felix out for a couple of days, and when Buddy needs to go out, he goes with one of us." Jake looked once more out the back door before shutting off the porch light.

"What do you think it was? You seem almost jumpy."

"Do you remember when I told you about the last case I worked on when I was a detective? The one with the guy from the track?"

"No, I don't think you ever told me about it," she replied, getting cold cans of soda out of the refrigerator. She handed one to Jake and sat down at the table. Jake stood looking out the kitchen window.

"There were these missing women, four of them. I traced it down to this guy who worked at the track. It was all circumstantial evidence, but he was convicted anyway. He had some mental health issues. After that, I left Granelle to go to seminary. I came back when the associate pastor position opened up at our church. Then six years ago, it started all over again," Jake turned away from the window and sat down at the table with Sarah. "Women began to disappear again. Kathy Stanwick was one of them."

"I had heard something about Kathy being a victim of a kidnapping," Sarah said. "It's taken her a long time to get through her fears. I know that we've been praying for her at the women's group again."

Jake nodded. "It was really hard on Kathy. When she was abducted, one of the kids in the church went missing too, and his mother died while looking for him that night. It turns out that he had been kidnapped by the same man. Reggie Bennett asked me to come back and help the police force track down the kidnapper. By then, four women and Sam, the little boy, were missing. We finally did catch up with the perp and found the missing women and Sam. We also found out that the kidnapper had been keeping some kind of a wolf... well, it was a big creature, part wolf and part something else."

"But it was a wolf, right?" Sarah asked.

"No. Not really. There was an old legend that told that this creature was part wolf and part werewolf."

Sarah laughed, "Werewolf? And people believed it?"

"I don't know what it was. But many people truly believed in this creature, including the man that kidnapped Sam and the women. It seemed to have almost a human intelligence. And Sam had some kind of control over it. I went to stop this creature and Sam stopped me. It ran away. I never saw it again. It just disappeared into the night."

"Do you think that's what I saw outside tonight?"

"I don't know. I hope not, because I'm afraid if that creature is back, something bad is going to happen in Granelle again."

Sam Craig sighed as he rolled over on the cot. It was a hot night, and he threw the light sheet off and looked over at the bed where his best friend, Johnny Mendoza, softly snored. So far, Sam's summer vacation with the Mendozas in Granelle had been boring. The two boys hadn't seen each other in two years since Johnny had gone down to Poughkeepsie to spend a week with Sam. This summer, Sam's father finally let him come back to Granelle for a visit. It had been years since Sam had been in the small town that lay just outside of Saratoga.

Stanley Craig, Sam's father, had originally said no to the visit. He never wanted Sam to return to the town that had been the place where Stanley's nightmares had come from. The same town where his son, who was eleven then, had been abducted by a man who was criminally insane, the same town where this madman had killed Sam's mother. Although Sam claimed that he remembered very little of that summer, Stanley was afraid of letting his son reawaken those memories.

But it had been a long time, and Sam was almost eighteen. Trevor Grant, the man who abducted Sam, was in prison facing twenty-five years to life. It was Anne, Stanley's fiancée, who convinced Stanley to let Sam spend a few weeks during the summer with his old friend. At least by going to the Mendoza's house, Sam would have some supervision.

Finally, Stanley relented after Anne broke down and cried after another fight with Sam. She was afraid that Sam would ruin her wedding if he wasn't allowed to spend the weeks they would be on their honeymoon with Johnny. Besides, Anne wanted to spend her first weeks as Mrs. Craig free from her troubled new stepson. The day after their small wedding, Stanley watched as Sam pulled out of the driveway for the two-hour drive north to Granelle. Stanley felt nervous and guilty, for like Anne, he wanted a few weeks of peace too.

Sam shifted on the cot again, turning toward the other wall. What bothered Sam the most was that his old best friend had turned into someone he didn't even know. Sure, Johnny always got the good grades before, but now he was in the drama club and band, and his friends were all the smart nerdy kids that Sam and Johnny had always made fun of. Sam realized that their old friendship was over, and this would probably be the last time they would be together. They were just too different now.

Sam looked over at his friend. Johnny's long legs hung off the bed, reminding Sam of just how tall Johnny was. Sam was the complete opposite of Johnny. Where his friend was tall, with short black hair and eyes, Sam was short, heavy in comparison, with long, dirty blonde hair and pale brown eyes.

Sam pulled out a pack of cigarettes that he had hidden in a knapsack under the cot. Quietly, he got up and went to the bedroom door. He listened to the sounds of the house. Hearing nothing, he snuck out of the room and down the stairs to the kitchen. His bare feet made no sound as he crept through the silent house.

Sam unlocked the back door, looked back over his shoulder, and went out into the muggy August night. He felt unease sweep over him as he stepped out onto the back deck. He looked around the backyard toward the deep woods surrounding the house. The moon was bright and lit up the yard, with deep shadows cast from the woods. The water in the large above-ground pool shimmered in the moonlight.

This wasn't the first night that Sam had snuck out to have a smoke after everyone else had gone to bed. But tonight, something felt wrong. He looked back inside the house, but no one was there. Sam stood listening to the sounds of the night. Finally, he shrugged and lit his cigarette. He sat down on the top step of the deck and took a long drag. Only a week into this vacation and Sam couldn't wait to return to Poughkeepsie. He really had wanted to go to

Saratoga and see the old historic town, but it was ruined when he saw the woman cop. With a rush, he remembered being locked in the basement with her, the creature, and Trevor's anger at Sam's failures. When he saw Meg, Sam remembered things he had long ago forgotten. Now, he wanted to get away from this house and this little town. There were too many bad memories that were closing in on him.

Everything Sam had hoped about this visit had been a disappointment. He had dreamed about coming back and seeing Melinda Yates again. His thoughts of her kept him going during some really bad times in Poughkeepsie. But she had changed a lot in the years that Sam had been gone. Melinda now called herself Lindy and acted embarrassed when she introduced Sam to her new friends.

Sam and Johnny even took a walk past the Craig's old house, only to find it had been remodeled. The detached garage was gone and replaced with a two-car garage that was attached by a breezeway. Sam couldn't help staring into the woods in the back of their old house, the place where his mother had been killed, where red eyes watched him at night, and where Trevor Grant had abducted him. And Sam didn't want to go to the old Hanson house at all. Just the memory of being held in that basement, where the creature kept watch on him, was enough for Sam. He didn't want to see that house again as long as he lived.

Sam finished his cigarette and flicked it into the yard. He pulled another one out of the pack and put it in his mouth. He looked up and gasped. From just inside of the woods, two glowing red eyes were looking at him. He got up, and the dark shape moved forward. Sam dropped his cigarette and ran for the door. Inside, he locked the door, then peeked out the window. The eyes were still there, watching him.

"Sam?" he heard a voice behind him. "Is everything all right?"

Sam turned to see Mr. Mendoza standing in the doorway to the kitchen. Sam took a deep breath to calm his racing heart. He glanced back out the window and still saw the red eyes looking at him. He remembered something from his past, about not telling anyone about the creatures. He stuttered, "Everything is fine."

Mr. Mendoza turned on the light and went to the refrigerator. "Are you sure? You seem a bit nervous."

"Yeah, I'm sure."

"Were you outside having your cigarette?" He opened the refrigerator and pulled out a container of juice. He got a glass out of the cupboard. Sam stood watching him, not sure how to respond. Finally, he nodded. Mr. Mendoza poured his juice, then looked at Sam with concern. He started to say something, but Sam bolted for the stairs, leaving Mr. Mendoza shaking his head.

Sam was too afraid to look out the window again. He curled up on the cot and finally fell asleep as dawn was breaking.

CHAPTER 3

It was a hot day and the humidity made it unbearable. The concrete yard where the inmates were enclosed seemed to give off more heat and offered no shade from the daunting sun. Most of the inmates sat on the wooden benches trying to catch a hint of a breeze. As oppressive as it was outside, it was worse inside with no fresh air and the heat baking the brick building.

Trevor Grant used his time outside to flirt with a female guard. He knew his handsome olive complexion, black wavy hair, and dark eyes were irresistible, and Melody Wilcox seemed powerless to his flattery. Melody was slightly overweight and kind of drab. Her longish brown hair was up in a tight bun which made her already round face appear more so.

Trevor smiled at her and played with a piece of her hair that had escaped the bun. His interest in her was focused on her new job responsibilities. She was now able to assign inmates to different jobs within the prison, and he was trying to get more time out of his cell. Trevor was waiting until the perfect time to convince her that his interest was in her and not what she could give him.

Knowing the hour was nearly over, Trevor leaned in and whispered something to her, making her look around for the other guards. Playfully, she pushed him and began to walk away, turning to smile at him as she did. He smiled back as another inmate walked up to him.

"Why you wasting time with her?" the inmate asked.

Trevor watched her until she stepped back inside the building. He then looked at his acquaintance. "Melody is very sweet."

The inmate laughed. "Sweet? Where have you been? She'll eat you for lunch. Looks like she already did!"

Trevor looked hard at him, and he stopped laughing. There was something about Trevor that scared most people. He wasn't big, nor did he threaten anyone. But in his look, most other inmates saw something evil. The inmate backed away and returned to the group that had been watching Trevor. Trevor looked at them all, making a few glance away nervously. The guards came out and led the inmates back into their cell blocks.

At first, the inside felt cool away from the daunting sun, but Trevor knew it was short-lived. Trevor hated the confines of the prison, having spent the majority of his life outside, living in wooded areas. He tried to make the best of it by being nice to the guards. He hoped to get a reduced sentence for good behavior. As they walked single file back to the row of cells, a guard was handing out mail as they passed.

Trevor watched the man in front of him get a handful of mail and continue on. The guard handed Trevor an envelope. Trevor looked surprised.

"Finally got something, Grant. Just keep moving," the guard said as he turned his attention to the next inmate.

Trevor looked down at the envelope as he walked back to his cell. Once his cell door closed, Trevor ripped opened the envelope.

> *Trevor,*
>
> *This is the most difficult letter I have ever had to write. When you were young, I had so much hope that you would follow me as the next keeper. I tried to care for you as if you were my own child and prepare you for the duties that this would require of you.*
>
> *When you refused to listen to me back when we first came to Granelle, I knew then that this would not work. I wanted to help you prepare a child that would take over after you, since I felt that you would be unable to care for a child. But your dislike of children led you to insist on Angelos. I wanted to give you a chance to prove yourself to the creatures, so I allowed you to bring him to the house. That was a dismal failure. All you did was expose the creatures to risk, causing that man to be committed to a life of darkness, and made us flee, causing years of setbacks and failures.*
>
> *I should have let the police find you then and start immediately to train another boy myself. But I had grown fond of you in my years of caring for you. I put your needs above the creatures, which should have been my first concern. Now, circumstances have caused the remaining creature to be alone. He is at mortal risk of exposure because of your failure to listen and my failure to put him first. Your incarceration makes it impossible for you to carry out the responsibilities. So, I have to make an alternative choice for the sake of the survival of the creature.*

Another has been chosen in your place. The boy will have difficulties, since he will not be prepared as he should. But the creature has selected him, and he will be told everything he needs to know when he is old enough to have no interference from adults. I have made all the arrangements and everything has been set into motion for this to be completed.

This letter comes to you now because I have died. I'm writing this letter to impress upon you the need for your continued obedience. I know that you have not spoken of things and that you have kept your vows of silence. The protection and safety of the creature is the most important thing now. Keep your silence...it will ensure your life.

Shamus

Trevor crushed the letter in his hand. Fury and grief shook his body as his love of Shamus conflicted with his rage over another person taking his place. This was *his* destiny, not another person's. His entire life had been sacrificed, and now he would not be able to carry on. He stood and paced the small cell, the letter held tightly in his fist. His eyes fell on the envelope on the bed.

Trevor snatched it up and narrowed his eyes at the return address. That coward Donovan had sent the letter. He knew that Donovan would have handled Shamus' affairs in the end. He threw the envelope and letter onto the bed and continued his pacing. He had to figure out who this boy was that would dare to steal his future. But he knew Donovan would never tell him, not unless he felt his life was in danger.

Trevor walked to the bars of his cell and looked out. Another inmate across the narrow hall looked up, then back to his book. Trevor turned around and leaned his back against the bars. The small cell seemed to close in on him. He had to find a way to get out and get back what was his. The dark rage clouded his thinking, but he fought against it, remembering what happened to Angelos. Trevor forced himself to remain in control and took several deep breaths.

"Grant, time to go to work," a guard said behind Trevor. "Back away, so I can open the door."

Trevor stepped away from the bars, grabbed the letter, and shoved it into his pocket. As he followed the guard down the hall toward the laundry room, he began to formulate a plan. The heat from the dryers hit Trevor as the guard opened the door to the laundry room. Melody was there with a clipboard talking to another inmate. She looked over as Trevor approached. The guard motioned to the other inmate to follow him out. Trevor glanced around as the door closed and didn't see anyone else there.

"Anyone else here?" Trevor asked.

Melody checked something on her clipboard and then nodded her head toward the other side of the room.

"Oscar's in there finishing up some folding. He should be done soon. The washers on the other side should be done. You can start there," she said as she continued marking the paper on her clipboard.

Trevor reached out and gently caressed her cheek. Melody looked up and then glanced at the other side of the room. He dropped his hand and went behind a wall to where the washing machines were lined up. The large commercial machines were filled with sheets and towels. Trevor began the monotonous job of emptying them into large canvas carts. He listened, waiting for Oscar to leave before making a move on Melody. He smiled as he thought of his plan.

About twenty minutes later, Trevor heard voices and knew that Oscar was being moved back to his cell. Trevor had several dryers running and was still transferring wet linens to the big dryers.

"Trevor, you have to be careful," Melody said as she came to him.

Trevor smiled one of his most charming smiles. He reached out and pulled her into his arms. "I know, but I couldn't resist," he murmured into her hair. She trembled as he kissed her.

Trevor pulled away from her and she started to say something. He put his fingers to her mouth to silence her. "I have something to talk to you about."

"I can't switch you to another job," she said with a little frown. "You just got put here a few weeks ago."

"It's not about a job," Trevor said looking toward the door. "Did you hear that I got a letter today?"

"You did? I thought you said you had no family," she said, trying to take his hand. Trevor allowed it and gave her a slight squeeze.

"Just an uncle, but he has died." Trevor tried to look sad.

"I'm sorry to hear that. Who was the letter from?"

"It was from his attorney. I'm his only heir."

"Oh, was he...?" She bit her lip.

"Yes," Trevor said looking down into her face. "Very rich. He owns property all over the world. It's all mine now."

"I don't know what to say."

"Imagine, Mel, if things were different. We could travel, see the world, live in luxury. There is so much money that we would never run out in our lifetime. Just imagine what we could do. We could live on a yacht or on an exotic island," or I could show you France. The romance of France is intoxicating – beyond most people's wildest dreams. And it is my homeland. How I'd love to show you the castle that is now mine."

Melody's eyes got big. Trevor imagined she was already discarding her dumpy apartment, the broken down car, and the maxed out credit cards. She looked at Trevor, and he could read her doubt.

"If things were different, you wouldn't look twice at me," she said sullenly.

"You're wrong. You don't know how difficult my life has been, what I've been subjected to. You have been a lifeline in this place, and I could show you a world that few people know."

"But look at me." She stretched her arms out.

Trevor looked into her eyes and took her hands, pulling her to him. "What I see is a wonderful person, who has done so much to make my life in here better. I only wish I could repay you somehow."

"What happens to the money now?" she asked in a quiet voice.

"I need to go back to Ireland to sign paperwork. But I'm in no position to claim the inheritance. If only, there was a way...."

"Who gets the money if you don't claim it?"

"I don't know. I suppose it will be considered unclaimed and the government could take it. If only there was a way that I could give the money to you. I just can't see how," Trevor said in a gloomy voice. Melody leaned against his chest for a moment, until Trevor moved away from her. "I'd better get back to work. I don't want you to get in trouble if someone should check on us." Trevor turned back to the wet sheets.

Melody stood watching Trevor put the wet linens into the dryers and then turned away. She went to the small office that was in the laundry area. She sat down behind an old metal desk and set the clipboard down. She thought of the movies she had watched of rich people and all the things they owned and how happy they seemed. Maybe, if there was a way she could help Trevor get the money, he would give her some of it, just enough to get out of this town and start over again. Even though Trevor denied it, Melody had no illusions about his affections. She knew that he wouldn't want her if he were free and had money. But with some money, Melody could be happy even without Trevor.

CHAPTER 4

The next morning, Sam and Johnny sat smoking in Johnny's tree house. The boys sat with their legs dangling off the edge, facing the woods. Johnny looked over his shoulder several times to make sure his mother couldn't see what they were doing.

Sam put out the cigarette and flicked it toward the woods. He was still shaken by the day before and pulled another cigarette out.

"You're going to smoke another one?" Johnny was astonished. Sam, said nothing, stuck the cigarette in his mouth, and stared at Johnny. He shook his head and lit it. Johnny ground out his cigarette and flicked the butt toward the woods. He glanced back toward the house and thought he saw his mother in the kitchen window. Johnny stood up and walked toward the other side of the tree house. He hoped to block Sam from the view of anyone looking from the house.

Sam turned around and faced his friend. Johnny wore his neatly ironed blue jeans with a polo shirt opened at the neck. His deep brown eyes were wide with an innocence that Sam lost years ago. Sam ran his hand through his long dirty brown hair. He wore his favorite ripped, stained jeans and an old T-shirt that had a rock band's name on it.

"Let's have some fun," Sam said standing up.

"We've been having fun," Johnny said crossing his arms. "Can you put that thing out before my mother sees you?"

"If I put it out, will you agree to do one thing that I want to do?" Sam asked. Johnny heard his mother call out to him.

"Yes," he hissed. "Just put it out. She's coming."

"Okay, okay. Chill," Sam said dropping the cigarette into his almost empty can of soda.

"Johnny," Mrs. Mendoza called out from the kitchen door.

"Okay. We'll be right in," Johnny yelled back. He pulled out breath mints and popped one into his mouth. He handed the pack to Sam. Sam sighed and took one, knowing that Johnny would get upset if he didn't. Sam learned from experience that the mints never really masked the cigarette smell. He knew from the looks that Mrs. Mendoza gave him that she knew he was smoking; Mr. Mendoza probably told her after he caught Sam last night. But she'd never believe her little boy would be smoking in the tree house too.

Mrs. Mendoza waited for the boys to come to her. "Johnny, I need you to run these over to the church. It's announcements for the newsletter and the bag of clothes for the clothing drive."

"Sure," Johnny said eagerly. "Can we pick up some videos for later too?"

"Okay. Here's some money... and come right back home. No side trips this time," she said firmly, looking at Sam.

Johnny took his mother's keys and they both went to the car. She stood watching as they pulled out of the driveway. She knew she'd have to talk to her husband later about Johnny's smoking with Sam.

Jake sat in his office at the church with his Bible on his lap, staring out the window. Many things had changed over the years since Walter Ryerson had left the care of Granelle Gospel Church to Jake. Pastor Walt had said that he wasn't retiring, just moving on. He told Jake that you can't retire from a call on one's life from God. Jake had learned so much from Pastor Walt. Even though many of the older parishioners didn't like the changes that Jake made when he became the senior pastor, they grudgingly admitted that Jake was reaching a younger generation.

Jake found the administrative part of the job tiresome, but he was content in the life he chose. He didn't regret giving up police work to be a pastor. And since he married Sarah, he felt a deeper sense of peace then he had ever felt before.

After last night though, Jake felt that peace had been shaken. Six years ago when Trevor Grant was sent to prison for murder and kidnapping, the police reported that Grant had had a pet wolf of some kind, and it was loose in Granelle. Jake had actually seen the creature and knew it was more than a wolf. He also knew that it was no pet of Grant's. It was the police chief, Reggie Bennett, who told the community that the strange dark creature seen wandering around Granelle was just a wolf, and it had gone back to the wild when Grant was taken into custody. Jake never bought that theory.

He closed his Bible and set it on his desk. Most people didn't believe in the powers of evil anymore, but Jake knew it existed. In his years as a police detective, Jake had seen it all. But it was in Trevor Grant and that creature that Jake saw the epitome of evil. The detective in Jake kept going over what Sarah thought she had seen, and he realized how long it had been since anyone had sighted the creature. Sure, over the years, a few adventurers hunted in the woods for the creature, but Jake knew they hadn't found it. One man even killed a wild dog and claimed it was the creature.

Most of the time, Jake dismissed the claims, but somehow he knew that this time it was back. Now sitting in his office in the quiet church with the sun spilling in from the window onto his desk, Jake felt a deep sense of foreboding. Even praying didn't calm the feeling that something was wrong. Jake picked up the phone and dialed an old, familiar number. As he listened to the phone ring, he wondered what he was doing. He quickly hung up before anyone answered. Jake turned back to his Bible and flipped to the book of Psalms.

He began to read when he heard a knock at the door. Penny Forester, the young blonde church secretary, opened the door and poked her head in.

"Pastor Jake, someone is here to see you. I know you don't have any appointments, but..."

"Who is it?"

"It's...he just wants to say hello." Jake tilted his head questioningly, and Penny stepped inside and closed the door. Penny's sparkling blue eyes were wide in fear.

"What's going on, Penny?" Jake asked.

"Do you know who that is? What is that man doing in our church, Pastor Jake?"

"Can you calm down and tell me who is out there?" Jake said, putting a restraining hand on her arm.

Penny closed her eyes and took a deep breath. "It's that guy. You remember him. Angelos, Doug Angelos. He's that guy you arrested for murder! Murder! He's here in our church. Why?"

"Doug is here?" Jake asked, puzzled.

"Yes, here in our church offices. You don't think he will try to murder us?" Penny's voice was filled with fright. Jake looked down at her and shook his head.

"Doug didn't murder anyone. Don't you remember? He was exonerated when Trevor Grant was captured six years ago."

"He was? I don't remember that."

"You were probably in college then. You said he wanted to talk to me?" Jake asked. Penny just nodded. "Why don't I just go out and talk to him at your desk. You can stay here and calm down a little bit." Jake paused at the door.

"Doug is not a murderer. He was wrongfully convicted."

Penny nodded and sank down into Jake's chair. Jake pulled the door closed behind him and saw the big man sitting in a chair by the door. Jake thought Angelos had aged since he saw him last. His greasy black hair was streaked with gray, and he was a lot thinner than Jake remembered. As Jake walked toward him, Doug stood and smiled.

Jake reached out and shook Doug's hand. "How have you been?"

"I've been really good, Detective." Doug stuffed his hands in the pockets of his jeans.

"I'm not a detective anymore."

"Yeah, I knew that. I just wanted to come say hello and let you know that I'm doing okay now."

"That's great. What brings you back to this area?"

"It's track season. I got my old job back when I got out of the institution."

"So, you're working with the horses again?"

"Yeah, I love the horses. As long as I stay on my meds, I'm okay. I've wanted to come before, but I was always too scared."

"Scared? Of me?"

"Well, not really of you. But the past...you know, it was really bad for a while, even after I got out of Coxsackie. I had really bad dreams and the voices, but the meds take care of all that now."

"Well, medication can be a good thing sometimes. Have you thought any more about what we had talked about when you got out of Coxsackie? About how God can help you?"

Doug shook his head, "God doesn't work for me. When I think about God, those voices start screaming in my head. Then, I get the bad dreams. I don't want the dreams. No offense to you. You helped me a lot when Trevor was arrested, but I can't do the God thing. The meds work good. Like I said, I was going to come see you the last bunch of years I was at the track. But I couldn't."

"You could have come at any time. I'm glad to know that you are doing okay," Jake said, as he put his hand on Doug's shoulder.

Doug dropped his head and smiled shyly. "I know it was okay with you. But not with them. Only this time, when I thought about coming out and letting you know I was okay, they didn't seem to care."

"Who, your bosses?"

"No," Doug said looking around. He whispered. "No, you know, the voices."

Jake felt disturbed by what Doug was saying. "Why don't we go in my office and talk some more?"

"No. No," Doug said. "I've said too much already. I was just supposed to come and say hi. I was just going to tell you that I was okay now. I've got to get back to the track now."

"The voices said it was okay to visit me?" Jake asked.

"I've really got to leave. I got a guy waiting to drive me back to Saratoga." Doug inched toward the door.

"Okay, I'm glad you decided to come and see me. It's good to hear that you're doing so well." Doug wiped hand across his mouth and then looked out the window to a truck that was sitting in the parking lot.

"Okay, okay. I'm leaving now," he said and walked to the door. Jake went to the window and watched Doug walk back to the truck. He began to pray for Doug, and as he did, Doug whipped around and saw Jake at the window. He looked scared, and he tripped. Doug grabbed for the door and yanked it opened. The driver said something, and Doug shook his head and gestured. The driver looked back at the church and waved at Jake.

Jake watched the truck backing up and saw a car with two teen boys waiting to pull into the lot. He recognized the driver as Johnny Mendoza and figured he was coming by to see Penny. Jake turned away and saw Penny back working at her desk. He went to the sanctuary, like he did whenever he just wanted to be alone and pray. It was something he did back when he first was an associate pastor and Pastor Walt had been hospitalized. He found it a place where he could just spend time with God. Jake sat down in a pew halfway down the aisle and looked up at the big cross behind the pulpit.

Closing his eyes, Jake felt the turmoil of being confronted with the past. Seeing Doug and knowing that the dangerous creature was wandering around Granelle reminded Jake of his failures. Jake had a hard time letting go of the mistake he made when he arrested Doug Angelos ten years ago for the murders of those four women. Because the wrong man was arrested, Grant was able to kidnap other people in this small town and even murder Clara Craig. Jake knew that Grant had killed Clara so that he could force her son to live a life in seclusion with the creatures, just like what had happened to Grant as a child.

Jake knew that Sam's life would be haunted by the murder of his mother and by his abduction. He also knew that Meg and the other women who Grant had hurt would never be the same either. Jake lived with the guilt of his mistake. He had tried turning it over to God again and again. Yet even with committing his life to working in ministry, Jake lived on the edge of self-condemnation. He tried to believe the verse in Romans that said "there is now no condemnation for those who are in Christ Jesus." He prayed that verse now, prayed for forgiveness for the arrogance he had in those days, prayed for peace, and prayed for each of those he knew who had been affected by Grant.

CHAPTER 5

As the day's heat and humidity built, a virus spread around the prison, leaving most of the inmates and guards sick. The laundry was short handed, with many of the workers laid up in the infirmary. Trevor had not been stricken and was working extra hours, which he didn't mind after he heard that Melody had been working extra shifts. Melody was unloading a big washer when Trevor came down. He went to help and let his hands linger over hers as they put the wet sheets into the dryer.

The phone rang on the desk, and Trevor watched as Melody ran to answer. Trevor smiled as he watched her. He knew she was getting anxious. Melody had tried to talk about the money to Trevor, but every time he brushed her off. He said it was pointless to discuss. He just wanted to be with her. They had been alone for hours over the past few days, and Trevor used every free minute to lavish affection on Melody.

But Trevor could see the greed in her eyes when she tried to talk about the inheritance. He told her the only way would be for him to go to Ireland, which was impossible. The last few days, he refused to even discuss the money with her. But he knew she was being drawn into the idea of finding a way to get Trevor to Ireland. He knew the only way that she would help him would be if the idea of his escape came from her.

Trevor pushed a cart to the dryers to unload them. This life was so far away from the way he used to live. Instead of existing in a tiny, sweltering cell, Trevor had flown around the world with Shamus, living in mansions on massive estates, dining in the best restaurants, wearing expensive clothes, and caring for the creatures. Trevor knew that the fortune that Shamus had was to protect the creatures. It had worked too, until they had moved to Granelle.

Trevor heard Melody's shoes on the concrete floor as he began to fold the sheets. He kept working as she came over to him.

"Trevor," Melody said, laying her hand on his arm. He looked up with a sad smile. "I need to talk to you about something."

"Okay," he replied. "Let me get this load going first."

"No," she looked around nervously then pointed to the outside door. "Let's step outside for a minute. I have an idea, and I don't want anyone to overhear us."

"Okay," Trevor said with a smile. He followed her to the door and she pulled out her keys.

"It's just..." Her voice began to quiver. She struggled to get the door opened and they stepped out into the hot afternoon. Trevor pulled her toward him.

"Just want to be outside for something different?"

Melody shook her head and pulled away from him. "We have to be serious now. I might have an idea to get you out of here. But I don't know if my plan will work."

"Oh, Mel, don't torment me like this." Trevor turned away from her.

"No, listen a minute."

"I don't want you to take any kind of risk."

"I want to do this. You say you love me, right?"

"Of course I do," Trevor said in a soft, affectionate voice.

"Do you really want a real life with me?" Her eyes searched his face.

"I cherish every moment we can be together. I'm glad you gave me the extra time these past few days."

"That's not what I mean. I'm talking about a real life, like living in the real world. We can never be any closer here than we are right now."

"Mel, we could get married."

"Married?" she said breathlessly. "You'd marry me?"

"Will you? I can bear being here if I knew that you belonged only to me."

For a moment Melody was speechless. Then she threw her arms around his neck. "Yes, yes, I will marry you! But not here."

Trevor hugged her back and smiled. She would do anything for him now. "What do we need to do to get permission from the warden?" he asked.

Melody pulled away a little, still holding onto his arms. "We'll get married once we are far away from here. Listen to my idea; it just might work. Oscar is in the infirmary. I already called upstairs and got permission for you to work the next shift."

"Anything to be with you longer," Trevor said nuzzling her neck. She giggled and pushed him away.

"Not now. Let me tell you my idea. Because of the virus, the warden has asked a private company to help us with all of the extra laundry. They're supposed to be coming during the next shift to pick up a truckload of dirty clothes. I know you're not cleared to work with the outside contractors, but the warden's already gone for the day. With so many sick, no one is paying attention."

"You want me to sneak out on the laundry truck? I don't think that will work."

"Actually, I thought you could use the truck as a cover. There are security cameras that point down to the bay where the truck will be parked. I'll have you help bring the carts of laundry to the truck. There is a spot where the cameras can't pick you up. Plus, if I stand on the side, I can block the camera too."

"Then what?" Trevor was impressed with her idea so far.

"I'll move my car over to the loading bay. I'll have my trunk opened a little. When I give you a signal, slip into the blind spot and get into my trunk. After the truck leaves, I'll call my boss and tell him I'm getting sick and need to go home. We'll be out of here hours ahead of the end of the second shift when they will come looking for you."

"Don't you think they will check your car when you leave?"

"They never check employee cars. They won't have any reason to."

"But when you call your boss to tell him you're sick, won't he send another guard down?"

"I'll tell him I'm closing the laundry since the contractors just left. They won't suspect me once they find you missing. They will check out the laundry company first. That will give us time to go back to my apartment and gather some of my stuff."

"There are so many things that could go wrong. I don't want to expose you to this risk." Trevor added a layer of deep emotion. "I love you too much."

"It will work. This time tomorrow, we can be married and on our way to a new life. Let's get back inside and keep working. I don't want to get anyone suspicious before the truck comes."

Trevor followed Melody back inside. This could work, he thought, as he went back to loading the dryer. By this time tomorrow, Trevor would be free to find that child who was stealing his life.

Several hours later, Trevor climbed out of Melody's trunk at her apartment complex. He couldn't believe it had worked, and no one had suspected anything. He had waited in her trunk for what seemed like hours before he heard her start the car. The ride was bumpy and he was hungry, but he was free.

Melody stood by the car anxiously looking around while Trevor closed the trunk. She took his hand and practically ran up to her apartment. Trevor knew he needed her for a little longer, since his part of the plan was just beginning to unfold. She fumbled with the keys as she tried to unlock her apartment door. Trevor took the keys from her hands and calmly unlocked it.

As Melody stepped into the cool room, Trevor handed her the keys and watched her drop them on a table with her purse. He knew she was scared, but not of him. That was going to be her biggest mistake. Trevor took Melody into his arms and passionately kissed her. She didn't resist as he led her to the small cluttered bedroom.

"Oh, Trevor," Melody said breathlessly. "We don't have time right now..."

"Slow down." Trevor began to unbutton her shirt. "You said they wouldn't suspect you."

As Trevor began to kiss her neck, she found she almost couldn't resist him. But she stopped him. "Let's wait until we get out of here. I don't want to get caught."

"How soon before they start looking for me?" He continued his planned seduction.

"Probably another hour. I still need to pack, and we need to make plans too."

"You did great getting me out. Now that we're finally alone, I just want you."

"Oh, Trevor, do you really mean that?" she said wistfully. His response was another passionate kiss.

A half an hour later, Trevor lay on the unmade bed watching Melody get dressed. She smiled at him as she pulled a suitcase out of her closet.

"You should probably get dressed too, Trevor, so we can get moving," she said.

"Where can I go in prison clothes?" Trevor said. Melody looked at him and stopped packing. "Once it gets on the news, I won't be able to go far in those clothes. What about money, too? We need enough for gas, food, and for a place to stay until I get some of my own cash."

"We can stop somewhere once we're gone," she said turning back to her suitcase. Trevor took her hands to stop her and get her attention. "We can't just stay here," she whined, making Trevor cringe. "We've been here too long already. We need to just leave."

"The problem is that I need to call Donovan and get some funds wired to me so we can leave the country. Unless you have enough money for tickets to Ireland...."

"I don't have that kind of money," she said sitting on the edge of the bed.

"Is there a store opened close to here?"

"There's one store that is open twenty-four hours."

"I need you to get me a change of clothes and find an ATM. Get as much cash as you can. This will be the only time that we can get any money. Once they start looking, we can't leave a trail."

"I have some cash in my dresser. We can just use that. I don't want to come back here."

"I didn't want to ruin the surprise I have for you. But..."

"What surprise?"

"Well, you did want to get married. I want to get married tomorrow, but I want everything to be perfect for you. And I really do need to call my attorney overseas. I can make those calls while you run out. I'll keep the light off and no one will even know I'm here. Just make it quick," he said in his most charming voice.

Finally Melody left and Trevor picked up the phone. He dialed the overseas number and waited. When the phone was answered, Trevor said, "I wanted you to be the first to know that I'm out of jail."

"Who is this?" the voice demanded.

"That's no way to talk to your client, Mr. Donovan. I got Shamus's letter, but you were remiss in including one from yourself."

"Trevor, I'm not your attorney. I have nothing to say to you."

"You better listen very carefully to what I have to say," Trevor said, his voice cold. "I know a lot about you. Things that the police would want to know. Now, you do exactly what I say, and your name will stay out of it."

"I don't trust you," Donavan shot back.

"Then it's best to not make me angry. First and foremost, where's the boy?"

"Shamus was very explicit in his final requests of me. You are not to know where Sam is living now."

"Sam," Trevor said, anger darkening his voice. "That worthless boy. That's the one that Shamus chose?"

Donovan quickly realized his blunder. "He didn't choose Sam. He just didn't want you to know where Sam lives," he stammered.

"You never were very bright, were you? Now, I need money," Trevor went on.

"What about Sam?"

"I'll take care of that. I'm sure my uncle made a contingency in his will for the protection of the creature should anything happen to Sam. What is it?"

"I cannot discuss this with you."

"You can discuss this with me now or when I get to Ireland."

"You'll never make it to Ireland. I'm going to call the police."

"And tell them what? That I called you? What good will that information do for them? I need money. I'll call you tomorrow with the information so you can wire it to me. Don't cross me, Donovan. I'll have you killed."

Trevor hung up. Sam, he fumed. All he needed to do was to get rid of that boy and he would be able to reclaim what he was entitled to. But first, he needed to get rid of Melody. She would be back soon with her demands. He would be ready to deal with her first, and then he would find Sam.

CHAPTER 6

Jake stood in the backyard cooking hamburgers for dinner. Sarah thought it would be great to eat outside tonight. Jake thought it was too hot, but she seemed so excited about the idea that he didn't want to hurt her feelings. Jake looked up from the grill to watch Buddy crashing around inside the woods. The wooded backyard provided the Petersons with privacy. Buddy came out of the woods with a stick in his mouth and dropped it at Jake's feet.

"Not right now, Bud," Jake said. Buddy whined and pawed at the stick. He looked up at Jake with sad brown eyes.

Jake laughed at the dog as Sarah came out the kitchen door. "How are those burgers coming?"

"Probably another five minutes or so," Jake said, looking down at the burgers.

"You know, it's hotter out here than I thought it was. Do you mind if we eat inside?" she asked.

"No. Whatever you want to do is fine with me." Jake smiled to himself.

Sarah went back inside and Jake finished up with the burgers. Sarah had the kitchen table set with fresh salad, hamburger rolls, and a variety of condiments. Once they were seated, Jake said grace.

As Jake fixed his hamburger, he inquired about her day. "So how was your trip to Saratoga? Did you get the supplies you needed to finish that painting?"

"Well, I had to special order some brushes, but they should be in next week. I stopped at Sorelle Gallery while I was there. They sold one of my paintings to a collector in New York. Sandy and Jean told me the collector might be interested in commissioning me to paint one for him, too. He really likes my work."

"That's great!" Jake said between bites.

"I'm so glad you told me to bring my work to Saratoga. I never thought it could lead to this."

"How was your other appointment?" Jake asked watching her closely.

"Well..." she began a little hesitantly. "Looks like I am pregnant."

"Should I get excited yet?"

"Let's wait. I've had so many problems with trying, the miscarriages, and the false positive the last time, I just want to wait a few months...or weeks before we get too excited. I'm so afraid of being disappointed again."

"Okay, but I'm feeling pretty confident this time," Jake said, taking her hand.

"Me, too," Sarah said with a smile. "But I want to wait before we tell anyone."

"You just tell me when. I can't wait to tell everyone we're having a baby."

"For now, we can tell everyone I'm officially an artist, now that I sold my first painting."

Jake and Sarah talked about her work and the baby while they finished eating dinner. They cleaned up the few dishes together and decided to take Buddy for a walk. It was still hot out, but the shade from the trees offered protection from the sun's rays. They enjoyed taking walks through their little neighborhood. Buddy pulled the leash as Jake tried to keep him from pulling him down the road.

"I've just about given up on him," Sarah said as Jake pulled back on Buddy again.

"Well, he is getting older. They do say you can't teach an old dog new tricks. When it was just me, it didn't matter if he was able to walk on a leash," Jake replied as Buddy once again pulled ahead.

"Yeah, you never trained him to sleep on the floor either. If he wasn't such a sweet dog, he would be impossible."

"Just like his owner, huh?" Jake pulled her close.

"Maybe." A car came up behind them, and Jake pulled Buddy to the side to let the car pass. But the car slowed and pulled up alongside of them instead.

"Isn't it too hot to be out walking?" Reggie Bennett asked as he rolled down the window. Reggie was originally from Manhattan and got his experience as a policeman working the harsh city streets. He was a big burly black man with a booming deep voice that he used to his advantage in police work. Well over six feet tall, Reggie worked out and was well-built from body building.

"Not too hot for us," Sarah replied.

"Been a while since I've seen you," Jake said to his former boss. As he leaned down to look inside the car, a blast of the air conditioner hit him. "What brings you out to this end of town?"

"Just checking in with a few people. Thought I'd swing by and see you, too," Reggie said. Sarah smiled at him and took Buddy from Jake. She and the dog walked up the street a few yards and then stopped to look at some wildflowers. Reggie watched her and saw how happy she looked. "Everything okay with you guys?"

"Sure is. Sarah just sold her first painting at Sorelle Gallery in Saratoga."

"Good for her," Reggie continued to watch her. Sarah began to gather flowers, but Buddy kept sticking his nose in her hands, trying to get her to pet him.

"How about you, Reggie? You seem a bit preoccupied. Is everything okay in Granelle tonight?"

"Sure. Everything is quiet here, and it's been that way for quite some time. I'll let you two get back to your walk. Looks like you're enjoying it."

Jake watched Reggie for a moment. "Are you sure everything is fine?"

"Sure. I'd better get back to the station."

"Okay." Jake straightened up. "Don't be such a stranger."

Reggie waved and pulled away. Sarah waved back as Jake caught up to her. He took Buddy's leash.

"What was that all about?" Sarah asked, putting her arm around Jake. They started walking back down the street to their house.

"I'm not sure. But I wonder if you weren't the only one to see that animal."

"Did you tell him I saw it?"

"No. I probably should have, but it hasn't been back. If we see it again, I'll give Reggie a call."

"Maybe you should call him anyway. If others have seen it, he might want to know." Jake didn't reply. He thought about Doug. "Jake, is something else wrong?"

"Well, I didn't want to say anything to you. It's nothing really."

"What's nothing?"

"Doug Angelos came to the church yesterday. He came just to say hello to me and let me know he was doing okay now. Angelos was that guy from the track that I arrested in the first case that involved those creatures. It's just strange, you know, his showing up right after you saw that animal in the yard."

"Why don't you talk to Reggie about it when you tell him about seeing the animal? He can check him out and make sure that there's no connection."

"Since when did you get so familiar with police work?"

"Comes from living with an ex-detective," she replied. "Besides, you seem so concerned about it. If there's anything to be worried about, let Reggie worry about it."

"Okay, I'll give him a call tomorrow. You know, Reggie was right about one thing."

"Yeah, what's that?"

"It's too hot to be walking tonight. Let's go get some ice cream."

"Sounds great to me. Let's take Buddy with us. He likes to ride."

Jake laughed. "He likes ice cream too. You spoil him as much as I do."

"Can't help it. He's really sweet, just like his master."

As they reached the driveway, Jake pulled his keys out of his pocket and they got in the car. Buddy tried to squeeze in the front seat between them, but Sarah firmly put him in the backseat.

As they drove away from the house, a dark shadow watched the car drive away. Once the car was out of sight, the shadow turned and ran off into the woods.

CHAPTER 7

Trevor drove Melody's car toward New York City after he disposed of her body. She had gotten him out of the prison, equipped with some clothes and cash. So now, he just needed her out of the way permanently. After he dumped her car, he would go somewhere safe where Donovan could wire him the money. Then he would find that boy.

Dawn was breaking when Trevor got to Brooklyn. He planned to dump Melody's car in a bad neighborhood so it looked like a robbery. Trevor found a spot to park the car on a side street. He tossed the keys on the floor and turned away. He walked several blocks to a subway entrance and went down the steps.

The platform was empty, and Trevor looked at the grid of the city, figuring out a route to Manhattan. There had been many trips to New York City when he lived with Shamus. Trevor loved Manhattan, but he didn't know the rest of the city well enough to navigate his way around. The train pulled up and Trevor stepped on as soon as the doors opened. The car was practically empty and he sat down, appearing bored.

As the train traveled underneath the city, the cars began to fill with commuters. No one paid attention to Trevor. Finally, he got up and followed several people out of the train. He walked several blocks to an Internet café and went in. He ordered coffee and a bagel, then turned his attention to a computer terminal.

The computer classes Trevor took at the prison came in handy as he searched the Internet. He was surprised to see his escape was already broadcast on the news. People would be looking for him with his accomplice. That was good for Trevor, since they wouldn't be looking for him alone. Trevor then started a search for "Stanley Craig" and was disappointed by the number of listings there were for that name. He narrowed his search to New York, but still had too many to check out.

Trevor sat tapping his finger on the table when the waitress refilled his coffee cup. He smiled at her briefly and then changed his search to "Meg Riley."

Again, the name was common and he narrowed it to Saratoga County. He was rewarded with a news article from last year on a private investigator that had helped win a big settlement for her client. The small picture of the investigator told Trevor that she was his Meg Riley. Trevor smiled to himself at the thought of Meg. He would enjoy toying with her again.

Again, Trevor did a people search. This time for "Jake Peterson" in Granelle, New York. The picture of the couple smiling in their wedding picture from two years ago intrigued Trevor. He had thought that the ex-cop would have married Meg. The petite woman who smiled up at her husband was so different. Trevor was intrigued. He remembered how much Jake had cared for Meg. Trevor read the article on their wedding and planned honeymoon. He went back and stared at the picture of the couple. Abruptly, Trevor deleted the browsing history on the computer and put some money on the table. He had time to make his plans. He wouldn't need to search for Sam Craig. His old friends would do it for him. Trevor stepped out into the morning heat. It was late enough in the morning for the commuters to be at work. Time for Trevor to get out of the city.

Trevor walked a few blocks up the street to an electronics store. He purchased a pre-paid cell phone. In the next block was a large parking garage. Trevor walked through the garage until he found a practically empty level. He chose a plain sedan and broke the side window to unlock the door. He searched the car, found a screw driver in the back seat, and slipping behind the wheel, he broke the ignition column and started the car.

Trevor drove out of the city and headed north. He stopped in a small town just before the entrance to the New York State Thruway that had a run-down motel, a small bank, and a few stores. Trevor smiled as he got out of the car and looked around. The town was just like Granelle, small and isolated, and no one would pay attention to a stranger passing through. He took the registration and insurance information out of the glove box.

Trevor walked into the little office and smiled at a girl who was dusting the counter. "Can I help you?" she asked, putting her cloth to the side. She was young and appeared very nervous.

"Yes, I'd like a room for the night." He leaned on the counter.

"Let me get my father. I don't usually check people in." She quickly left the room and went into a back apartment. A few minutes later, an older man came out. Trevor saw the resemblance to the young girl. His undershirt barely covered his large stomach. As he walked to the counter, he pulled up his brown shorts.

"Looking for a room?" he asked.

"Yes, for one, maybe two nights."

The man pulled out a registration card and said, "You need to fill this out. I need a major credit card and your ID."

Trevor frowned. "I just left the city and someone stole my wallet this morning. I don't have my credit cards."

"Oh, that's a problem," the man said hesitating.

"Not really though. I've been in contact with a friend. He's going to wire me money. I can pay for two nights now in cash. When I get the money, I'll give you some extra for your trouble. I have my car registration I can use for identification, too."

"Do you have enough for three nights?"

"I only plan on staying, at the most, two nights," Trevor said thinking of the small amount of cash he had on him. "I only have a little cash that wasn't in my wallet."

"You got enough for three nights and I don't ask any more questions," the man said narrowing his eyes at Trevor.

Trevor didn't like the way the man was looking at him. He had carefully put the money into a few small bunches before he left Melody's apartment. Trevor reached in his pocket and pulled out one small roll of money. He counted out some money and laid it on the counter.

"This will work. Just make sure when you leave you check with me again. I want to make sure I get that extra cash from you, too. I don't want to remember your face, if you get my meaning."

"No, I don't know what you mean," Trevor said with a tight voice. His anger was rising, and he tried to push it down.

The man looked down at the registration card. "Well, Mr. Jacobs, I saw a news report today. You look a lot like that guy that escaped from that prison in Elmira. I'd rather tell the police nothing than tell them that I think the stranger that showed up was Trevor Grant."

"What makes you think I'll let you get away with that?" Trevor asked his voice dangerous.

"This is a very small town, Mr....Jacobs. I just told my daughter, who also saw you that she could take a few days off. She works so hard for me and I thought it would be a nice treat for her to spend a few days with her best friend. Anything happens to me, she will remember every detail of you. We might be small town folks, but we aren't ignorant."

"I'm not here to cause trouble for you or this town. I just need a place to wait for some money to arrive."

"That's not a problem. I'd be happy to oblige. You can have it wired right here to the hotel, and I'll vouch for you with the bank...for another small fee."

Trevor hated this man and the way he was being played. But he needed that money from Donovan and needed it all to happen far away from Elmira and Granelle, in case someone was trying to follow his trail. He finally nodded. "Okay, but if you double cross me, I'll come back and kill you and your daughter."

"You won't have to worry about that, as long as you leave me a nice tip. I could care less about you or your life."

"Can I get the room key now?" Trevor asked.

The man smiled and handed him the key. He took the money off the counter and put it in his pocket. He picked up the registration card and looked at it as Trevor turned to go to the room. "As for this card, I'd be happy to give it back to you when we settle your account. I'd hate for this to turn up in the wrong place."

Trevor just glanced back at the man and then went back outside. He found the room that matched the key and let himself in, still seething. It was hot in the room and he turned on the small air conditioner. It groaned and clanked as it started up. The air it generated was only a little cooler than the hot air in the room. Trevor made his call to Donovan.

"Bobby," Trevor began his voice steely. "Are you ready to meet my demands?"

"Against my better judgment, I will send you some money," the older man replied. Trevor could hear the strain in his voice.

"You better be very careful that there is no trail to me. If you give me away, I'll hunt you down and kill you."

Donovan laughed. "If I wasn't such a coward, I would have already killed myself. Killing me would be a gift."

"Don't be a fool, Bobby," Trevor said, his anger growing again. "I'll..."

"Stop trying to intimidate me, Trevor," he cut in. "This isn't about you. This is about the creatures and protecting the legacy. You don't need to worry about me betraying you. But my loyalty is not to you. It's for Shamus and the creatures."

Trevor jumped off the bed and clutched the phone to his ear. "How dare you," he shouted. "You are nothing but a weasel..."

"Be careful what you say to me. I owe you nothing. The only reason I'm going to send you a cent is because of Shamus and how he cared about you. Now just give me the information for the transfer."

For a few moments, Trevor just stood shaking. He bit back his words and calmed himself. It would be foolish to let this money slip through his hands. Trevor took a deep breath and gave Donovan the information for the wire transfer. Donovan asked few follow-up questions and then hung up.

The heat was almost unbearable in the small motel room, but Trevor didn't want to risk exposure by going anywhere. It was bad enough the owner of the motel recognized him. It would take a full day for the wire transfer to come in and he had to wait. Turning on the television, he settled in to wait for the money and made plans for his trip north.

CHAPTER 8

Meg sat in the cool parlor of her client's mansion, listening to the woman cry. It had been a few fruitless days of following the woman's husband around Saratoga. He had been seen with an attractive younger woman, but Meg didn't catch them doing anything. Her client wanted desperately out of her marriage, and a cheating husband would have provided a nice alimony. But Meg couldn't produce what didn't exist.

After spending the last hour with the woman, Meg understood the husband's constant absence from the house. Meg knew it was time for her to just let this case go and move on to her next client. She let her thoughts drift to her newest case. She was already intrigued by it. A well-known businessman in town believed that his wife had been having an annual affair with one of the horse owners who came to Saratoga for the season.

This summer, the affair had become public and news of the indiscretion was making its way through the community. Her client had had enough and wanted to divorce his wife. It would be a high profile case, and Meg knew it could take her career to new heights. She figured she could just hang out at the track for a few days and get the necessary proof of the affair.

Meg was shown out by the housekeeper and decided to get right to her new case. It was already past post time, so the streets weren't as congested with tourists. Parking near the gate was just about impossible, but Meg had a friend who lived near the track. She parked in her friend's driveway and walked over to the main entrance. The track was packed and Meg looked around the grandstand. She reached in her purse and pulled out the snapshot of her client and his wife. A thin, rough-looking man, pushed past Meg and she turned and watched him as he headed to the other side of the track where the horse stalls were located. Just a backstretch worker, she thought.

The man who pushed past Meg walked quickly to the horse stalls. His friend, Doug, was brushing one of the horses for an upcoming race.

"Hey, you got mail," the man said. Doug stopped brushing the horse and frowned.

"Who'd send me mail, Juan?" Doug took the envelope.

"Got me," Juan said. "Someone who doesn't know where we live."

Doug stared at the return address and got a bad feeling in the pit of his stomach. The letter had followed him from two previous addresses before finding him at the track. He tossed the envelope on a bale of hay.

"Ain't you gonna read it?" Juan asked, picking up the envelope.

"Feels bad," Doug said turning his attention back to the horse.

"What'd'ya mean?"

Doug shook his head and felt heavy condemnation. Voices screamed in his head, and he hunched down away from the sound.

"Hey, Doug, you okay?" Juan sounded concerned.

"No, it's bad. Can you get my meds?"

"Sure, hold on." Juan went into the barn and came out with a bottle of pills. He dumped some in Doug's hand and handed him a bottle of water. Juan watched as Doug took the meds. "You think the letter did this?"

"Yeah." Doug held his head.

Juan picked the envelope back up from where he had tossed it. He looked at the return address, but since he couldn't read English, he couldn't tell who it was from. He ripped open the envelope and looked over the hand written letter. "What's it say?"

Doug took the letter and tried to focus on the words. "Shamus is dead," he said in a flat voice.

"Who's that?"

"Just some guy I knew a long time ago. I have to get out of here."

"Okay, I'll drive you. Let's burn it first."

"The letter?"

"Yeah. Maybe it'll help you."

Juan took the letter from Doug and stuck it in a metal bucket. He pulled out a lighter and lit the pages. Doug watched as they turned brown and curled in the small flame. But it did little to calm the screaming voices. Juan watched his friend and then went to the next stall. He told another guy to help with their horses and took Doug's arm, leading him to the old battered pickup truck.

As they drove away from the track, Doug sat with his head in his hands, willing the medication to work. Doug didn't pay any attention to where they were headed, but the further from Saratoga they drove, the better Doug felt.

"You feeling better yet?"

"A little bit. Thanks, Juan."

They drove for a while in silence. Doug sat with his head back, feeling the effects of his medication. He had already taken it that morning, so this extra dose was making him feel lethargic and extremely tired. Doug dozed in and out while Juan drove the old truck around the back roads.

After about an hour, Juan woke up Doug. "How you feeling? I'm getting hungry. We can get pizza there."

Doug looked up and saw a small pizza place on his left. He nodded and Juan pulled the truck into a spot right in front. Doug frowned as he fumbled with the door handle.

"Where are we, Juan?" Doug asked. He was feeling a bit panicked.

Juan saw Doug's reaction. "It's okay. We're in that town where you saw that preacher." Juan watched as Doug walked over to him. A woman came down the narrow sidewalk and scowled at the two disheveled men. She recognized the one, but didn't place him right away. As they walked into the pizza place, she looked back at them.

Doug and Juan walked in and ordered a pizza. They sat in a booth and waited for their food to come. Juan made small talk while Doug held his head. He didn't feel very good, and the smell of the food was upsetting his stomach. He wanted to get out of Granelle, and he felt a certain dread fall over him. The voices didn't help, as they continued their relentless attack on Doug.

After they ate, they left Granelle, and Doug begged Juan to take him to their rented house instead of back to work at the track. He had sleeping pills at the house that would shut out the voices and the horrible feeling he had that something bad was about to happen.

A feeling of foreboding swept over Jake as he sat at his office in the church. He picked up the phone and called Sarah.

"Hey, babe," Jake said as she answered the phone. "What are you up to this afternoon?"

"You checking up on me?" Sarah teased.

"You know me better than that," he replied, feeling relief at her carefree response. "I just felt like I needed to call you. You okay?"

"I'm fine. Felix is fine. Buddy is fine. Well, Buddy is fine now that he's on the floor and not the couch. So, how's my overprotective husband? Are you fine, too?"

Jake laughed. "Yeah, I'm fine, too. I was just worrying...I can't help it."

"Jake, I'm fine. I just got back from the grocery store. I'm just putting away a few groceries. I'm going to put stew in the Crock Pot and then I'm going to paint."

"That sounds great. I've got a late counseling appointment so I might be delayed getting home."

"That makes stew a great dinner then. It's ready whenever you get home, honey."

"I'll call you before I leave. By the way, did you check with the doctor about painting while you're pregnant?"

"I'm using watercolors today. Nothing toxic. Trust me. I'm not going to do anything I'm not supposed to do, and I'm going to follow the doctor's orders to the letter."

"I'm sorry to second guess you. I just had a strange feeling a little while ago."

"Like what?" Sarah asked.

"It was nothing. I guess I am just still feeling uncomfortable since seeing Doug."

"Speaking of that...did you ever call Reggie and let him know that Doug came by the church?"

"I tried this morning, but he was out. I'll try again after I get off the phone with you."

"Well, in that case, I'll let you go. If I don't get the stew started, it won't be done, even if you're late. I'll talk to you later. I love you."

"Love you, too," Jake said, hanging up. He dialed the police department and left a message with the dispatcher for Reggie to call him at the church. Penny knocked on Jake's door and came in with a few things to go over with him. With the distraction, Jake didn't think about calling Reggie back until he was heading out the door to go home. But first, he made a quick call to the house. A feeling of dread washed over him as the answering machine picked up his call.

CHAPTER 9

Trevor stood at the kitchen of an abandoned camp house at Lake Desolation washing his many bites and cuts with peroxide. The fight had been difficult, but it was worth it all. For the first time in days, Trevor felt in control again.

Since Donovan only gave him a small amount of money and the motel owner took a large cut, it left Trevor short on cash, requiring him to change his original plans. He had dumped the stolen car downstate and took a different one. He also stole a few boxes of a sleeping aid from a store. It wouldn't have the affect the old drugs had, but the access he used to have to the prescription drugs was gone.

The old camp house was the last thing Trevor wanted to live in. But again, he found his options very limited. He was sure people were looking for him. Even if he was able to find a rental with track season going on, he couldn't take the risk of someone recognizing him. So he found an abandoned camp house at Lake Desolation. It was far from the road and was pretty run down. But it was a place close enough to Granelle so he could take care of his old enemies, but far enough away where no one would find him. .

Once Trevor was satisfied with the house, he took a ride to Granelle. Hiding the car in the woods, he walked until he found the Peterson house. It was in a new development that Trevor wasn't familiar with. The access from the woods wasn't easy, and he knew he would need to be careful of watchful neighbors. The next part of the plan, however, was one he had done many times in the past. Breaking into the house and being in position to abduct his next victim would be simple. When Sarah's car pulled up, Trevor hid in the woods and waited.

Trevor watched her putting away groceries and saw her answer the phone. When she got off the phone and started cooking, Trevor cautiously entered the house through an unlocked window. He quickly subdued Sarah in the kitchen, but he didn't count on the dog. Buddy attacked Trevor while Sarah lay unconscious on the floor. It was a fight to get Buddy locked in the closet in the kitchen. Trevor was left with several deep bites. With the dog barking and growling from the closet, Trevor picked up Sarah and carried her out of the house.

Back in Lake Desolation, Trevor laid Sarah on a filthy bed in the small bedroom near the kitchen. She began to stir as he tied her to the headboard. The gash on her head had stopped bleeding, but she still seemed dazed. Trevor picked up a filthy cup that had water and dissolved pills in it. He forced it between Sarah's lip and she weakly struggled. He managed to pour some down her throat. He stayed watching her for a while until she settled back into a drug-induced sleep. These drugs would have to work for now. Once he reclaimed his inheritance, he would do things the proper way.

Jake was frantic when he searched the house and couldn't find Sarah. He heard Buddy clawing against a door and found the dog locked in a closet. Jake knew Buddy had been in there for a long time, based on the depth and number of claw marks on the door.

With a feeling of dread, Jake picked up the phone and dialed the police department. When the dispatcher answered, he asked for Reggie. She tried to find out what Jake wanted, but he just insisted on talking to the captain. She wouldn't put his call through until Jake told her to ask Reggie if he would talk to him. Finally, Reggie picked up the call.

"Bennett," Reggie's gruff voice said.

"Reggie, this is Jake," Jake's voice broke.

"What's wrong?"

"It's Sarah. She's gone."

"For how long?"

"I don't know, Reggie. But Buddy was locked up in a closet."

"Could she have gone out?"

Jake hesitated, feeling broken. When he finally answered, he had managed to hold his feelings in check. "Reggie, I'm not an ordinary civilian here. My wife is missing. There's a big mess in my kitchen. Buddy was locked in a closet. Her car is in the driveway...."

"I'll be there in ten minutes. Don't touch anything." Reggie hung up without saying anything more.

Jake sunk down in a chair in the living room and listened to Buddy whining in the garage, where he had put the dog so he wouldn't contaminate the crime scene. Ten minutes later, Buddy's barking let Jake know that Reggie had pulled into the driveway. Jake stepped out onto the front porch. As Reggie got out of his unmarked police car, a police cruiser pulled up in back of him.

Reggie barked instructions at the two uniformed officers as he walked up to meet Jake. Jake was relieved to see Reggie and wanted to just break down. But the cop in him knew that he had to hold it together and give Reggie all the information he could.

"Jake," Reggie said, as he walked up the two steps to the porch. "Where should they start with forensics?"

"Probably the kitchen. It looks like Sarah put up a fight in there. There's a little utility closet in the kitchen that Buddy was locked in."

Reggie reached past Jake and opened the storm door. He waved Jake out of the way as two officers that Jake didn't know walked into the house. Reggie led them to the kitchen while Jake hung back. He watched as they pulled on rubber gloves. Reggie opened the closet where Buddy had been and looked at the gouges in the wood. Jake turned away and went back out onto the front porch. He looked up at the sky as the blue was slowly fading into a bright orange sunset. He breathed the night air and prayed.

Jake sat down on the top step, waiting and praying for Sarah's safety. He wanted so much to call Penny at the church and get a prayer chain going for Sarah, but decided to wait and see what Reggie thought first. Finally, he felt a hand on his shoulder, and Jake looked up at his former boss.

"Okay, now I need to find out everything you know." Reggie walked down the steps to stand in front of Jake.

"I talked to Sarah this afternoon. She had just gotten back from grocery shopping and was putting everything away. I told her I was going to be running late for dinner."

"Did you tell her what time you thought you would be home?"

"I told her I would call when I was ready to leave the church."

"Did you?"

"I tried, but she didn't answer. I knew something was wrong then, because Sarah is always where she says she'll be."

"Is there any chance she went somewhere? A friend's house, family?"

Jake was already shaking his head no. "She would have called to tell me."

"You know I have to ask you this...were you having any marital problems?"

Jake just stared up at Reggie. "Look, you know us. We weren't having marital problems. In fact...I tried to call you today about..." Jake hesitated. "Sarah thought I should have told you the other night. Now...why didn't I just tell you?"

"What is it Jake?"

"Doug Angelos came to see me at the church. He said he came to let me know he was doing okay now. It was just strange because just the night before, Sarah saw that creature in the backyard. She thought maybe other people in town had seen the creature and that we should tell you about it."

"So, you think Angelos had something to do with Sarah not being here?"

Jake stood up and stepped down to the sidewalk. "I don't know. How co-incidental is it that Doug shows up in Granelle after all these years and then Sarah disappears? And what about that creature coming back to town? Don't you think this is strange, Reggie?"

Reggie didn't respond. He pulled out a small notebook and pen out of his pocket. He wrote down a few things. Jake stood waiting. Reggie looked up. "Where did he say he was staying?"

"It's track season. He's in Saratoga with the horses."

"Jake, there's no easy way to tell you this. I got a call this morning from the Elmira Police Department."

"About Doug?"

"No, it's Grant."

Jake reached out and grabbed the railing of the steps. He felt it hard to breath. Reggie reached out and steadied him. "What?" Jake asked.

"Grant broke out of prison a few days ago. He got a letter from Ireland and it set him off. He's been having a romantic relationship with one of the female guards. She helped him escape."

"When were you planning to tell me? Grant hates me and you don't think it's important for me and the safety of my wife to tell me that Grant is on the loose?"

"Jake..." Reggie faltered. He shook his head. "I just found out a couple of hours ago. I wanted to tell you in person."

"I could have protected her. She could have been with me at church or I could have sent her to stay with her family in Wyoming. I would have gotten her out of Granelle."

"There is no indication that Grant is in the area yet."

Jake just stood staring. He didn't know what to say. He turned away from Reggie and took off toward the driveway. Reggie ran up and grabbed his arm to stop him. "Where are you going? We need to get searchers..."

"Where do you think I'm going, Reggie? Where did this all go down before? Where would Grant take his latest victim?"

"You don't know it's Grant. It could even be Angelos."

"Sarah is missing. Regardless of who took her, there's only one place that I can think to go to. I'm going to the Hanson house."

"No, you're not going, Jake. You can't compromise this investigation."

"You can't stop me."

"Yes, I can."

"She's been gone at the most for two or three hours. I need to find her, Reggie. Grant isn't going to waste time collecting other women, unless he's after Meg, too. He's just going to kill her. This is personal and you know it. How can you even have the audacity to stop me from going to the Hanson house and see if my wife is there?"

"What if you're right, Jake? Do you want to be the one to find her body?"

The two men stood glaring at each other. Jake pulled away from Reggie and yanked his keys from his pocket. His car was blocked in by the police cruiser and Reggie's car. Reggie followed Jake to the driveway. Jake just went to his car and fumbled with the door lock.

Reggie called out to him. "If you're determined to go, I'll go with you."

Jake stood looking at Reggie for a minute, and then nodded. He got in the front seat of the unmarked cruiser as Reggie got in and started the car. Reggie called into the station and let them know he was headed to the Hanson house, discreetly leaving out that he had a passenger.

They rode in silence for a while. Finally Reggie spoke. "When we get there, I go in alone."

"No," Jake replied, his voice steely.

"I know you. This isn't a nameless victim. This is your wife. You are not going in, even if I have to handcuff you to the car. You will wait until I've searched the house. If I find her, I swear to you Jake, I'll come right out and get you."

Jake sat staring straight ahead and then finally nodded. "I need to call my secretary and get people to start praying for her."

"You need to wait...." Reggie started, but Jake interrupted him.

"Look, I know how much to say without divulging things that will hurt your investigation. I need to know that people are praying for her safety so I can leave her in God's care."

Reggie glanced at Jake. "Hard to believe you've gotten more religious."

"For years, I've prayed that you would have a personal relationship with God. Any other time, I would take the bait. But I can't right now. God forgive me. But I can't have a theological debate with you right now." Raw emotion washed over Jake. His love for Sarah tore at his heart.

"Make your call," Reggie said.

Jake pulled a cell phone out of his shirt pocket. He dialed the church number and waited. When the machine picked up, he hung up and dialed a different number.

"Millie, this is Jake," Jake's voice broke. "Sarah's missing....No, I'm with the police. Yes, just like before. Please....Thank you. I love you guys, too...Yes, I'll call when I know more. Bye."

Jake hung up the phone and put it back in his pocket. He looked out the side window as they reached Dunning Road. Jake knew this route well from those days six years before. The first house on the corner was the Craigs' old house. Jake spent so much time there with the family when Sam's mother had been killed. But it was at the end of this road, the old Hanson house. The run-down house sat alone in the dense woods at the dead end. It sat abandoned since the days that Grant had used it to hold his prisoners.

Reggie pulled the car into the driveway and Jake looked up at the old house. Years of neglect had left the house sagging and weather beaten. Jake just sat in the car while Reggie got out and walked up to the porch. Now, sitting in the driveway, Jake knew he couldn't have gone into the house, even if he wanted to. He somehow knew it was empty. Reggie wouldn't find Sarah or anyone else. Reggie looked into a filthy window and saw the old furniture covered with sheets. He walked up to the front door and listened for a moment. He glanced back at his old friend before he entered the house. Reggie drew his service revolver and stood listening for a few long moments. Thick dust covered everything, and Reggie could tell that no one had been inside for years. Even so, he quickly searched the house.

Reggie knew intuitively that the kidnapper was Grant, although he also figured that Angelos and that dark creature were involved too. And even though Jake didn't work for him anymore, Reggie cared deeply for Jake and his wife, and he would handle this case personally. Reggie stood at the door for a moment, thinking about Jake's comment about Meg. That was going to be a problem. When Meg Riley had been a cop, she was insolent and abrasive. Reggie knew he was going to have to call her and tell her about Grant's escape. It was not a conversation he wanted to have, but he knew the call had to come from him.

Reggie left the house and got in the car. He didn't say anything to Jake as he settled behind the wheel. There wasn't anything to say. They both knew that the cycle was starting again. It was a quiet drive back to Jake's house.

CHAPTER 10

That same evening, Meg watched her client's wife walk up Broadway with another man. Following discreetly behind, Meg tried to blend in with the crowds on the street. Her cell phone rang and she quickly pulled it out to answer it. She glanced at the caller ID and frowned.

"Riley," she snapped.

"This is Captain Bennett," the voice responded.

"I'm working right now, Captain. Can I call you back?"

"What I have to say won't take long."

"Well, I don't work for you and I need to go."

"Meg," Reggie said softly. "Something's happened that you need to know about."

Meg abruptly stopped walking, causing the man behind her to bump into her. She didn't even notice as he apologized. "Meg? You've never called me that."

"Can I come see you?"

"Captain, just tell me what's going on."

"I'm just calling to notify you that Grant escaped from prison."

"When?" she demanded.

"A few days ago."

"Why did you take so long to call and let me know?" Meg asked, quickly scanning the crowd around her. Fear gnawed at her. "Hoping he gets to me first?"

"Riley, that's uncalled for. I just found out a few hours ago and am notifying you so you can be careful."

"I was home alone at my house all weekend. He could have been there."

"We have no evidence that he is in the area or that he was headed this way."

"How did this happen?"

"I'm not at liberty to discuss the case with you."

"I'm coming to Granelle right now. You're going to tell me everything. I want in on this."

"No. This is not even our case. And if it was, you wouldn't be in on it."

"Oh, why's that, Captain? You asked Jake to come back and consult on a case once. But I can't come back? I at least stayed working in the field. I'm a PI now and a good one, too."

"That's not why, and you know it."

"What's the problem then?"

"You really want me to say it? Your work record wasn't very clean when you left. Need I remind you...?"

Meg hung up on him. She wasn't going to let him get away with dismissing her on the phone. She would just go to Granelle and force him to give her answers. Meg looked around the crowd again and realized that she had lost sight of the woman she had been trailing. Heading up Broadway, she got into her car and headed west. Anger and fear spurred her as she took every shortcut she knew to avoid the still bustling summer traffic. Once outside of the city, she floored the gas pedal, flying past houses and through stop signs.

Yanking opened the front door of the Granelle Police station, Meg walked right past the dispatcher, who tried to stop her. The dispatcher followed her to the squad room, telling her she wasn't allowed back there. Meg headed directly to Reggie's office but was stopped by Greg Matthews.

Greg had just come on the force around the time Meg was fighting with Reggie over the old cases. Greg was still the youngest officer on the force. He wore his hair in a short crew cut and had big blue eyes that showed his innocence. Everyone in town treated Greg like a kid, and he wasn't very well respected, so he developed an attitude and wore his uniform even when he wasn't working. He thought the tough act would garner the respect he felt he deserved. "Out of my way, Greg," Meg said, glaring at him.

"That's Officer Matthews to you." Greg puffed out his chest.

"I'm here to see Bennett. Don't get in the middle of this."

"Riley, you can't just waltz in here like you own the place. You want to talk to Captain Bennett, you can make an appointment. Or you can talk to one of the officers so they can find out what your problem is first."

"My problem? You want to hear my problem, Greg. I'm here because I talked to Bennett about half an hour ago. He called me. Now get out of my way."

"Big talk from..." Greg started.

"Enough, Matthews. Go find someone to give a ticket to." Reggie stood in the doorway of his office. "I take it you have something to say to me, Riley."

"What gives you that impression?" Meg said, pushing past Greg. She walked into Reggie's office and sat in one of the chairs. Reggie closed the door, pulled a chair away from the wall, and sat down next to her. "Look, I should have called you this afternoon when I got the call, but I got called out. I wanted you to hear about Grant from me, not some officer you don't even know."

"I should have been told as soon as you knew. Grant probably still wants to kill me. What was more urgent than calling me right away?"

"You aren't the only one who needed to know about Grant. I talked to Jake and the other victims as well. And there's a possible local lead in the case."

"Still, there's no excuse for waiting hours, Captain. I could have been abducted."

"You're right. But you know now."

"I want in. You can't keep me from investigating."

"Yes, I can. You would never be objective in this case, and you know it. This is too personal. I can't have you get involved in this."

"I'm a private investigator."

"Who hunts down cheating spouses. I read the papers. But, it goes beyond the personal vendetta here."

"Oh, I get it. You don't like it that people who work for you have opposing views from yours. I remember that, too. But, I was right. Those creatures were real. The myths were true too. Trevor was the keeper of those creatures. It was just too weird a theory for you, so it was wrong."

"Those 'creatures,' as you like to refer to them, are just wolves. Where is the evidence that anything besides wolves truly exist? There is none."

"I saw him with my own eyes. So did Jake and Sam. We all told you what they were. Plus there was the forensic evidence."

"You told me what Grant told you they were. But there is no evidence of any type of other species. It was just an overgrown wolf."

"How can you be so blind?" Meg groaned in frustration.

"And this is why you can't come back and work for the department. I'm still in charge. I know how you must feel..."

"No, you will never know how I feel. Did that monster break into your house? Did he hold you captive? Don't sit here and tell me you know how I feel. You don't have a clue how I feel."

"Okay." Reggie stood up and put his chair back.

"Now tell me," Meg said, crossing her arms.

"What?"

"What happened? How did he escape?"

"Okay, I'll give you that. It's going to be all over the news anyway. He got some letter from Ireland and it set him off. He was in with one of the female guards. She snuck him out in the trunk of her car."

"I hope they nail her."

"She's dead," Reggie said, sinking into the chair behind his desk.

Meg stared at him for a moment. "Excuse me?"

"They found her body buried in a shallow grave in the woods behind her apartment complex. Probably wouldn't have found the body for a while, but they had heavy rains down there. Washed away the loose soil and exposed the sheet she was wrapped in. Couple of kids found her."

"When did they find her?"

"Just today. That's what prompted them to finally call and warn us."

"Has anybody traced where he has been?"

"This is Elmira's case. We are cooperating with their investigation."

"What do you mean? You're not doing anything here? Have you been to the house?"

"Yes, I have. He hasn't been there. No one has in years."

Meg sat and thought for a few long moments. Reggie was watching her, and she realized he was answering just enough questions that she might just go back to Saratoga and not cause any problems in Granelle.

Finally she spoke. "Is there anything else I should know?"

"No," Reggie said.

Meg studied Reggie for a minute. "I think there's something you're not telling me." Reggie just shrugged and leaned back in his chair. Meg knew that meant he was finished, and he wouldn't tell her anything else. "The letter. What was the letter about?"

"No one knows."

"How can that be? He's in jail. Don't they read the prisoners' mail?"

"It was from an attorney's office. They don't open letters from attorneys."

"Did they at least contact the attorney to find out what it was about after he escaped?"

"I don't know," Reggie said, trying to remain patient. He was starting to get annoyed by all the questions. He was usually on the other side of interrogations. "Look, if I hear anything else, I'll be in touch. That's all I have for now."

"You really expect me to believe that?"

"You have no choice," Reggie said flatly. He got up and walked to the door of his office. He expected Meg to follow him, but she didn't. Making a disgusted noise, Reggie left her sitting there and went to the break room.

Meg sat thinking, waiting for him to come back. She strained to see what was on his desk, but caught Matthews glaring at her from the squad room.

Finally, she stood and left. She got back to her car and decided to check out a few things in Granelle.

Driving through the small town, Meg felt a little bit of nostalgia. She loved this little town, but it didn't love her. No matter how hard she worked, she never felt she measured up to her male colleagues. It all started with Reggie. When she got that forensic evidence that an animal was tied to several cases in Granelle and overseas, he wouldn't listen to her. The forensic evidence showed it was the exact same animal, not just a similar animal. When Meg tied it all to an old Irish legend, Reggie told her stop wasting time.

Meg had known she was right and continued to pursue her leads. When Reggie found out she disobeyed his orders, he suspended her. Even when that creature was found and all the evidence proved Meg had been right all along, Reggie never let it go that she hadn't followed his orders. His attitude affected her working relationships with everyone on the force and extended to the district attorney's office. Even today, Greg Matthews' treatment of her showed her that nothing had changed.

Meg stopped her car in front of a little real estate office. Mo Reynolds was Meg's best friend from high school and the only licensed real estate agent in Granelle. Meg stepped into the cool office and a young receptionist looked up expectantly.

"Hi, I'm here to see Maureen Reynolds," Meg said, smiling.

"Did you have an appointment?"

"No, I'm an old friend."

"Well, Ms. Reynolds is out of the office right now. If you want to leave her a message, I'll have her call you when she gets back?"

"Can I wait for her?"

"Oh, I don't really expect her back. She's tracking down some information for a new client."

Meg nodded, "Okay. Can I leave my card for her?"

The girl nodded. Meg jotted a note on the back of the card and left it on the counter. The phone rang and Meg left as the girl answered the call. She stood on the sidewalk looking around the small town. Not much to it, just a few stores, a few places to eat, a bank, and a few churches. Meg squinted up the street toward the gospel church. There were a lot of cars there, and she wondered what could be going on at church on a weekday that would bring so many people out.

Meg decided to drive over to Dunning Street and check out the old Hanson house for herself. As she drove past the church, she wondered about Jake and his new life. Meg was surprised to see a group of people standing on the side lawn of the church. She'd ask Mo about it when she talked to her later.

CHAPTER 11

As the afternoon sun shone in the windows, Meg sat in her office staring out onto the street below. She watched people walking down Broadway, hoping for a glimpse of Grant. She had given up on her client's wife. In fact, she had no interest in her work at all. Several times, her assistant tried to get her to talk, and Meg blew her off.

Work wasn't the only thing that was suffering either. She wasn't returning calls to her family or friends. It was now in the news that Grant had escaped and his accomplice had been killed. Meg figured they were all calling to find out information from her that the news wasn't reporting. But she didn't know anything more than they did.

Meg kept a constant vigil around her. Several times that morning, she followed a dark haired man through a store or up the street only to find that when she caught up with him, he wasn't Trevor. Meg had a new security system put in at her house that was wired directly to a monitoring company. She even instructed them to call the police first and then call her. Her paranoia held no boundaries.

Her cell phone rang, taking her out of her reprieve. She looked at the caller ID and saw it was her father again. She hit ignore to silence the ringing. Meg stood and went to the window. She watched a couple walking toward Congress Park and realized it was one of her clients. Her phone rang again and Meg went back to see the caller ID.

"Hello," Meg said feeling her heart flutter. This was the call she had been waiting for.

"Ms. Riley?" the voice asked.

"Yes," she said a little breathy.

"This is Arty Stone."

"I've been waiting for your call."

"Yeah, took me a bit to get some info. I checked with my contacts here in Elmira. I don't know what your guys are saying up there, but there's nothing going on down here. The chick he was with had a bag all packed. Her car is long gone. Don't even know what direction he went when he left the area."

"Did you find out what kind of car it was?" Meg said, grabbing a note pad.

"Yeah, it was a '95 Ford Escort. It's light blue and really beat."

"Have they checked for it?"

"Dead end. I figure if he's as smart as you say, he probably ditched it already. Looking for it is going to be a waste of time."

"Well, it's my time isn't it? I need to find out where he was headed."

"I'll check with gas stations and find out the last time was that she got gas. If the tank was low, he would have had to stop somewhere. But it's a long shot. How far do you want me to go with this?"

"Arty, this is my life I'm trying to save, not a deadbeat spouse. So there's no limit. Find me something downstate so I can figure out who his target is. If you want some money now, fax a bill to my office."

"You've helped me with some PI work, so I'm willing to help you out, especially 'cause it's personal. But if you're willing to go that route, I can pull a few guys in to help me search if you want to pay for them."

"Go ahead and do that. And, since you're going to be hiring anyway, do you know anyone in Poughkeepsie? I'm running into a stone wall there too."

"What's in Poughkeepsie?"

"Some kid I want to find. His name is Sam Craig."

"I might know someone there. I'll check and see if he's free. Anything else about this kid I should know?"

"He was the kid in the Grant case, the one that was abducted with me. I just need to find him."

"I'll get back to you soon," Arty said hanging up the phone. Meg went back to her vigil at the window.

Jake followed the other searchers through the thick woods around Granelle. The heat and humidity were practically unbearable, but everyone seemed to press on hoping for some sign of Sarah. Many of the volunteers were from the church. While there were many volunteers in the woods, others were at the church making meals for the searchers, handing out flyers with Sarah's picture, and just praying for Sarah and Jake. Several of the women in Granelle Gospel's ladies' auxiliary had already been to Jake's house to do dishes and leave his supper for him. Jake appreciated the love and kindness of the people in this little town.

But Jake also knew that this was a waste of time, just like before. They weren't going to find Sarah any place in the woods. It was just something for people to do to feel like they were helping. Even though Jake knew it was hopeless, he, too, couldn't stay away from the search, just in case she was found.

Several times, Jake saw Reggie with a group of searchers. Jake had tried to talk to Reggie a few times, but Reggie held him off and wouldn't talk to him. Jake knew that this was the way he handled family members during an investigation, but he was annoyed to find Reggie treating him like he was just an ordinary citizen. Jake knew that he was going to have to confront Reggie at the police station soon.

"Pastor Jake," someone called out. Jake turned to see one of the teens trying to catch up to him. He stopped and waited. "Penny sent me here to find you. Lunch is ready and you have an appointment coming up in a little bit."

"Thanks, Randy," Jake replied. "I'll head back to the church."

"Mind if I walk back with you?" Randy asked.

"Come on." They headed back toward the church, walking in silence for a while. Randy was part of the church's youth group. He was almost as tall as Jake and really skinny. He had red hair and red freckles across his nose.

Finally Randy asked, "Do you remember Sam Craig?"

"Yeah, I got to know his family pretty well just before they moved."

"I was a year younger than him, but I remember him from school. A bunch of us were wondering if you think what happened before is happening again."

"No one knows for sure."

"One of the guys said you used to be a cop. Is that true?"

"Yes, but that was a long time ago."

As the church came into sight, Randy pressed for more information. "After talking to the other kids, I thought maybe ..." Randy hesitated. "I really like your wife. She's really nice to me.

Randy stopped walking as they got to the church parking lot. The lot was packed with cars. Jake stopped too. "What do you really want to ask me, Randy?"

"I know this is coming out all wrong," he said, hanging his head.

"Just ask me. It's okay."

"I'm worried for my little brother. He's about the same age Sam was when he was taken. Do you think that maybe this is personal, like because you were a cop? Or do you think this is happening again? Do you think that another little boy is going to end up like Sam?"

"To be honest with you, I don't know. I'm not involved in the police investigation. Just keep an eye on your little brother and make sure he doesn't go anyplace alone. That's good advice no matter what's going on."

"I really am sorry about Mrs. Peterson."

"I know you are."

"I'm going to keep helping out looking for her. I work at the video store in town and brought some of the flyers there."

"Thanks. I'd better get into the church so I'm not late." Jake looked over at the church. He saw Reggie coming out of the woods and heading toward his car. Jake hurried over and caught Reggie just before he closed the door.

"Hey, I've been trying to catch up with you," Jake said. Reggie looked up.

"I've got to get going, Jake," Reggie said gruffly.

"I know you're really busy with the investigation. But I just wanted to ask you a few questions."

"I don't have time right now."

"Give me a time. Whenever you can make time, I'll come to the station. I have to know something."

Reggie sat, looking up at Jake. Finally he nodded. "Okay, come by the station tomorrow around this time. I'm following up on something now. Maybe I'll have something to talk to you about."

"Thanks, Reggie," Jake said with relief in his voice.

"Don't thank me yet. Sarah still isn't home and I'm not sure if this lead will pan out."

Reggie didn't wait for a reply. He shut the door and started the car. Jake turned and walked into the church. Reggie sat watching him, feeling frustration and sadness for his friend. He opened a folder that was on the seat next to him. Reggie wondered if the old mug shot of Doug Angelos still resembled him. He pulled away and headed toward town. He hoped the kid at the pizza place would recognize the man in the photo. If so, Reggie would finally have a solid lead in Sarah's disappearance.

CHAPTER 12

The next day, Jake sat waiting in Reggie's office. He understood Reggie's position of not wanting Jake involved in the investigation of Sarah's disappearance. But Jake did not like being treated like he wouldn't understand the investigation. He had heard that Meg had been turned away by Reggie as well. The turnover in the police force in the past few years had made it difficult for Jake to get any information unless it was from Reggie.

Reggie came in and closed the door behind him. He sat down behind his desk and looked at Jake with a face full of compassion and understanding. Reggie seemed to not know where to start. Jake waited for Reggie.

Finally Reggie cleared his throat. "Jake, I understand this has been a difficult time for you. We have been doing everything we can to locate your wife. The state troopers will be leaving the search at the end of the day. We will keep a small detail..."

"So, you're going to treat me like I'm an idiot."

"Now, look here," Reggie said. "You're the one that keeps hanging around."

"Six years ago, you asked me to come back and join the investigation."

"That was six years ago. A lot has changed...."

"But I thought we were still friends."

"You know that I can't allow friendship...."

"You know me better than that, Reggie. Why do you always let your pride get in the way of listening to people?"

Reggie started stammering but offered no reply.

Jake continued. "My church and the other local churches are all still going to keep looking for Sarah, no matter what you plan to do 'officially.' Meanwhile, have you have found out anything more about Grant? Have you checked with Mo Reynolds to see if any other houses have been rented in the area? Where is he holding her?"

"Don't tell me how to run an investigation, preacher," Reggie shouted. His voice carried out into the squad room, and Jake saw a few officers glanced toward the office through the large glass window in Reggie's office.

"I'm a trained investigator myself, Reggie. I could easily get a job on any police force in the area."

"Not without MY recommendation."

"Reggie, I'm not looking for a job on the force...it's just...Sarah is pregnant. I just found out the day before she went missing. We had been praying for a child, and now that it's a possibility, I...I need something to hold on to. Hope, Reggie. I need hope that she is going to come home. That was something I never realized that people wanted when I was a cop. They just want hope, something tangible to hold on to. You don't think I know that it's getting hopeless? Every moment that goes by, there is less chance of her being found. It already feels like she's been gone a lifetime."

"There's no proof she was abducted."

"See? There you go again, treating me like I don't know what's going on. We both know that Grant took her. We know his M.O. I know his M.O. He holds them until he has enough victims, and then he kills them all."

Reggie stared at Jake, then pulled a file out of his desk drawer and leaned forward as he opened it. He flipped through a few sheets.

"There are no new rentals in Granelle. No one has seen Grant in the area, but there are a lot of tourists in Saratoga right now. Saratoga Springs Police Department is looking in town, but it's almost impossible to check everyone out. We have checked out Angelos though. We think that there might be a connection to Sarah's abduction. He was seen by a few people in Granelle the day that Sarah disappeared. He even asked one person where you lived."

"So, you're thinking it's Doug?"

"He has a record and no one has seen him in days."

"Okay, but what's your theory?"

"Haven't fully figured it out," Reggie mused. "But maybe he's still in contact with Grant. Maybe he abducted her for Grant. Who knows, maybe that's how it happened when Angelos was involved with Grant before."

"Or have you considered that Grant might be setting up Angelos to take the fall again? I know for a fact that Angelos didn't have anything to do with those murders."

"No, you don't. No one does, except Angelos and Grant. Neither one will tell you the truth. People saw Angelos in town eating pizza with a Hispanic male the day that Sarah disappeared. He came back to Granelle a few days after he saw you at the church."

Jake stared at Reggie. He finally shook his head. "I don't believe he would have anything to do with this. He was in jail when all this happened six years ago." Jake sat thinking for a few minutes. "Did you talk to him?"

"Not yet. I've been having trouble locating him. Another reason to suspect him."

"Yeah, maybe," Jake was suddenly distracted. "Thanks for the information. It will stay between us."

"Stay away from the investigation, Jake."

Jake just nodded and stood up. He reached across the desk and shook hands with Reggie, who was left with a puzzled look on his face.

Jake looked at the big clock in the squad room as he left the station The drive to Saratoga seemed to take Jake longer than usual. Once in Saratoga, the cars were bumper to bumper to get into the track. Jake parked his car on a side street and walked to the track entrance.

Jake stood in line to go through the gate, paid the entrance fee, and walked around the track to the stables where the horses were. He asked a few people for Doug, and finally, someone pointed to some men preparing horses for their races.

Jake walked over to a man who was brushing a bay mare. He looked up at Jake. "Help ya?" the man asked.

"I'm looking for Doug Angelos?"

"Cop?"

"No, I'm a friend," Jake replied.

"He ain't got too many of them. Who are you?"

"Jake Peterson."

The man regarded him for a moment, the nodded going back to brushing the horse. "You the one that Doug went to see? In that town? That preacher?"

"Yes, that's me."

"I'm, Juan, the one that drove him."

"Do you know where he is today?"

"He in trouble?"

"I don't know. Do you?"

"Think so," Juan replied. "Cops looking for him. He got weird mail that sent him over. Probably on a bender."

"Where would he go? I know he's been doing well lately. Where would he go if he was going to get drunk?"

The man squinted at Jake and then shrugged. "We got us an old dive up by Saratoga Lake. People think track peoples all got money. Not us."

"Can you tell me what you and Doug were doing in Granelle a few days ago? It's really important that I know."

"Nothing really. Just having pizza. Cops already asked me this stuff."

"Would Doug have gone there?"

"I don't know. He hasn't wanted to go since he got out of jail. But he might."

"I need to talk to him. Can you tell me where that house is?"

"Up where Brown's Beach used to be. There's a dirt road, leads down to some old camp houses. Can't miss it. It's got junk cars in front, dirt brown, number's 505."

"Thanks. I'll try to find it."

"Gonna try to save his soul, preacher?"

"If I can," Jake said, smiling. The old guy laughed as Jake walked away.

Fifteen minutes later, Jake was sitting in front of a run-down camp house wondering if Sarah was inside. He wished he carried a gun. He got out of the car and walked to the front door. As he approached, he could hear Doug inside talking to someone. But the voice was muffled, and it sounded like Doug was crying.

Jake didn't bother knocking. He tried to turn the door handle and it was locked. He quietly crept to the back of the house. Doug's voice was louder from the back and he was crying loudly. He cautiously peeked around the back of the house and saw nothing but woods. Jake crept up to the back door and glanced into the window. He saw Doug sitting at the kitchen table alone. He was holding a handgun and crying.

"No. No," he kept mumbling.

Jake saw the liquor bottle on the table. He reached out and turned the door handle, a bit surprised that it was unlocked. He quietly slipped in the door. Doug turned in his chair and pointed the gun at Jake.

Jake opened his hands to show he didn't have anything. "Doug, it's me, Pastor Jake. I just came to talk to you. Can you put the gun down?"

Doug sat stunned, and then shook his head. "No use. It's too late. I just want to die."

Jake inched toward the table. "Listen, there's no reason to take your life. Whatever has happened, I'll help you."

"You can't," Doug screamed. "Shut up! I will get him to leave!"

"It's the voices again, isn't it? Well, I know someone who can get them to shut up."

"No, no," Doug whimpered. He put his hands over his ears, pointing the gun up at the ceiling. Jake took the chance and lunged for the weapon. Doug didn't have a good grasp, and Jake easily took the gun away. Doug groaned and dropped his head on his arms. Jake laid his hand on Doug's shoulder and began to pray.

As Doug began to calm down, Jake leaned over and softly asked, "Is there anyone else here?"

"What?" Doug said looking up.

"Are you alone?"

"Yeah. How did you do it? How'd you get them quiet?"

Jake pulled out a chair next to Doug and sat down. "I prayed for you. I asked God to silence them and bind them so they couldn't put voices in your mind."

"God? God made the voices be quiet?"

Jake felt anxious to find out anything about Sarah, but knew he couldn't miss this opportunity to share his beliefs. "I believe He did. The Bible says that when we are Christians, we have authority over evil."

"So, if you leave, the voices will come back?"

"You can have that same power, Doug. You don't have to live with this anymore. When you ask Jesus to forgive you for your sins, He comes in and lives within you. That evil cannot stay where Jesus is."

"But how, how...?"

"You just need to pray. 'If we confess our sins, he is faithful and just and will forgive us our sins and purify us from all unrighteousness.' Would you like me to pray with you?"

Doug shook his head. "They won't like it. I can't pray."

"I can pray with you. It might make it easier for you."

Doug seemed calmed by what Jake was saying. Finally Doug asked, "Why did you come? You didn't just come here by accident."

Jake shook his head and replied, "No, I came looking for you. My wife is missing."

"You think I know something about it?"

"The police do. They said you were in Granelle the day she disappeared. I thought it was strange since it seemed so hard for you to come just to see me. When I heard that you came back again yesterday when Sarah disappeared, I knew had to find out from you. Do you know anything about it?"

"No. The voices starting tormenting me after I visited you." Doug shuddered. "The meds had stopped working."

"Why did you go back to Granelle after our visit?"

"Juan was just driving me around. Sometimes, when I get out and just ride around, it helps me. I didn't know he was driving to Granelle until we were in town. He said he was hungry and we stopped for pizza. Then we left and he drove back to our place. Then Juan went back to the track because he had to take care of the horses."

"Could Juan be involved with Trevor?"

"Trevor? You think Trevor took your wife?"

"Yeah, I do."

"But he's in jail."

Jake sadly shook his head. "No, he broke out a few days before Sarah disappeared. Doug, what do you remember about Trevor? How did you get involved with him to begin with?"

"He came to the track one day. Just showed up at the stables. He was looking for someone to do a job with him. He flashed a lot of money around. I was living drunk most of the time then, and the money seemed good. But the horses were really scared of Trevor. It was like they sensed something on him. I took the work anyway. I helped him clear stuff out of the basement at that house. Then we brought down doors and I helped him make these little rooms. I didn't know what he wanted to do with them. I took the money and went on a good bender. When I finally sobered up, I was in jail for murder."

"When did the voices start bothering you? Around that time?"

"Yeah, I had been working at the house. Trevor left me there to pour some concrete, and that's when that animal came in. There was this old man living with Grant who was doing something with the crate in the back. Did you know about the old man?"

"He's in prison in Ireland," Jake said.

"No," Doug said, shaking his head. "I got a letter from him. He's dead."

"How'd you get the letter?"

"From his lawyer. It was only supposed to be sent when he died."

"Can I see it?"

"When I started reading it, the voices started screaming at me. Me and Juan burned it."

Jake thought for a moment and then it clicked. A letter from Ireland is what started this whole thing. Grant also received a letter in prison. "Go on, Doug. What else happened with you before?"

"Well, that old man said something to the animal and it bit me. It pinned me right in a corner and sat watching me. I screamed, and the old man just stood there, too. Like they were waiting to see what would happen to me. I stood there for a long time, shaking, too scared to do anything. Those animals were awful with big teeth. Finally, they got bored and just left me. I ran away and never came back to the house again. I was drunk for a long time, and then you arrested me."

"You were set up by Grant. I think that he's trying to set you up again."

"What can I do? I don't want to go back to jail."

Jake got up and looked around the tiny camp house. Doug just sat waiting for Jake. Finally, Jake came back to the kitchen. He leaned up against a counter. "Why didn't you ever tell anyone what you just told me?"

Doug was a little taken aback by the question, but shrugged. "When you arrested me, I was confused. I had been drunk for a long time. When I started sobering up, the voices began to taunt me. I went through the DT's, and the withdrawal was awful. I kept having nightmares about those animals. Sometimes, it was like I could see what they could see. The chaplain at the jail told me he thought I had a demon. I couldn't even say Trevor's name. It was like I couldn't form words. I was living a nightmare."

"You keep saying animals, plural. We only saw one."

"There were two, a boy and girl. Old man said they were mates." Doug shrugged. "Do you really think Trevor's got your wife? Do you think he'll try to come after me?"

"It's possible. He probably thinks you are irrelevant though."

"What's that mean?"

"That means that he probably doesn't think you are important. You don't live here, and Trevor probably wouldn't figure you would talk about him now."

"Should I talk to the cops now?"

"You're going to have to. They've been looking for you. Why don't you come back with me to Granelle now? I'll call Reggie Bennett. If he has any questions, you can answer them at my house. Then we can figure out what's next for you."

"You mean that? You'd really let someone like me into your house?"

Jake smiled, "Yeah, I want to talk to you more about God. Come on, we can talk more at the house."

Jake waited while Doug gathered his meager belongings. Together, they poured two bottles of liquor down the drain. Jake took the gun and locked it in his trunk. He figured he'd turn it over to Reggie when they met with him later.

CHAPTER 13

Reggie sat in Jake's living room glaring from Jake to Doug, listening silently as Jake told him about going to find Doug. Jake and Doug seemed more excited about Doug's making a decision to ask God to forgive him than anything else, but Reggie couldn't care less about Doug's conversion. He was livid with Jake for acting so rashly, and he sat stoically waiting until they both stopped talking.

When it seemed that Doug finally wound down, Reggie asked his questions. "Quite coincidental, isn't it, that you show up here just when Peterson's wife disappears?"

"We explained all of that," Jake said.

"So you say. I should bring you up on charges, Peterson. How dare you sit in my office and pry information out of me, then go over to Saratoga?"

"I explained that to you, too, Reggie."

"Don't you call me Reggie. Only my friends call me that," Reggie was shouting now. Jake cringed, knowing he deserved this. "I explained to you why I didn't want you involved in this investigation."

"You don't understand what it feels..."

"You're right. That's why you shouldn't be getting involved. You've allowed your personal feelings to impede this investigation. I'm trying to help you, Peterson. Don't you get that?"

"Yes, I do, but instead of speculating, you should have gone to the track and found Doug."

Reggie interrupted. "Do not tell me how to do my job! Oh, how coincidental is it that you just happen to find religion now?" he said, turning to Doug.

Doug dropped his head. "That's not fair, Captain," Jake said, defending Doug.

"Did you even think that his suicidal ideation could have been faked?" Reggie said, getting up. Doug looked up at Reggie, and Reggie nodded. "Played this poor preacher, who only has thought the best of you, for a fool, tell him what he wants to hear so he'll alibi you? Is that what you did, Angelos?"

"No," Doug said, lowering his head again.

"Probably his friend that you talked to at the track calls him, tells him that crazy preacher is hunting him down. Not only does he play act the whole thing," Reggie turned to Jake. "But you've told him everything that we know. He knows he's been seen in town the day Sarah disappeared, he knows about Grant, while we only know what he wants us to know."

"That's not the way it is." Jake stood to meet Reggie's glare. "This was real. It would have been easier for me if he did have her. But he doesn't. We've been talking for hours. There is no way he could have been pretending with me that whole time."

"Expect nothing more from my office. We will continue to investigate Sarah's disappearance, but you show up at the station, I'll have you locked up."

Reggie then turned to Doug. "You might be in the clear with 'Pastor Jake,' but not with me. You were involved with Grant before, by your own admission. Now, you show up here, and one of our citizens goes missing."

"I had nothing to do with Mrs. Peterson being gone," Doug said. "I'm really sorry that she is gone. Trevor's a bad person. That's all I know."

Reggie grunted. "And you're not?"

"Captain," Jake said in a cautious tone. "I'll vouch...."

Reggie changed the subject. "Where's Angelo's gun?"

"In the trunk of my car," Jake replied. "But, I want...."

"No, just the gun," Reggie said, pushing past Jake to go to the door. Jake followed Reggie out to the driveway and opened the trunk. Reggie pulled on some gloves, picked up the gun, dumping it and the bullets in an evidence bag, which he shoved in the squad car's glove compartment. Reggie got in the car and turned it on. Jake stood to the side watching him as he pulled out of the driveway.

When Reggie pulled into the police station three minutes later, he was still angry. He yanked the handgun out of the glove box and headed into the station. He noticed several officers still standing around drinking coffee. He yelled at a couple of the men to get to work and stormed through the squad room toward his office. He was not prepared to see Meg sitting in his office looking at papers on his desk.

Coming up behind her, he yelled, "Just what do you think you're doing, Riley?"

Meg jumped and set down a paper she was reading. "Waiting for you."

"That's not a good idea right now." Reggie snatched the paper Meg had been looking at off his desk. Seeing that it was a forensic report on a different case, Reggie dropped it and sat down in his chair. He put the handgun in his desk drawer, figuring he'd put it into evidence when she left. Meg sat down in the chair in front of his desk.

"I said, not a good idea right now."

"Well, when? When would be a good time to come back and talk to you about Grant?"

"Try this: not until I call you with some information."

"I'm a sitting duck. You've got to know that. I need information. What else is going on?"

"Nothing else," Reggie said. "I've already told you that he has not been spotted in the area."

"What are you doing? Have you checked...?"

"What about nothing else don't you understand? Get out of my office. I'll call you when I have information."

"I just want to help. Give me my badge back, just for this case," Meg said.

"You have got to be kidding. There is no way I will ever give you a badge."

"I need to help, Captain. I'm going crazy in Saratoga. I keep staring out my windows thinking I see Grant."

"No. You cannot objectively be on this case."

"But, Captain."

"I've had enough today. First Peterson, and now you. You both have to stay out of my way or I'll have you arrested. Next time I find you sitting in my office reading confidential stuff, I will. Don't test me on this, Riley. Now get out!"

Reggie took the gun out of his drawer and left his office.

Meg got up and started walking through the squad room to leave, and heard Matthews laughing. She looked up and he was looking directly at her. She felt humiliated, knowing he heard Reggie throwing her out. The drive back to Saratoga only enraged her more. When she got to her office, she didn't hold a bit of her anger in. She walked in and slammed the door so hard that the window rattled. Allison looked up from the phone at her boss and told the caller she needed to go.

Meg glared at her as she hung up the phone. "I'm here now, so you get off the personal call. Why not go ahead and keep talking? Just make your calls right in front of me."

Meg walked right up to Allison's desk, not realizing she was out of control. "That was Captain Bennett from Granelle, not a personal call, Ms. Riley," Allison replied in a cool voice that betrayed shock at Meg's rage.

"You expect me to believe that?" Allison nodded and swallowed. "Then why get off so quickly? Why not just keep talking? Oh that's it...you were talking about your boss behind her back."

Meg started to storm away, but Allison's quiet voice stopped her. "I don't like working for you anymore."

Meg whipped around. "What?"

Allison stood and confronted Meg. She raised her voice. "You told me about what happened between you and Captain Bennett. You promised you would never treat me like you were treated. But these past few days, you've been terrible to me. You accuse me of not doing work and taking personal calls, and you get mad at me for other people not calling you back. I know all about what's going on in Granelle, but you don't work there anymore. Go back to chasing down cheating spouses."

Meg just stared at Allison, feeling stunned. Allison had never spoken up to her in all the years she had worked for Meg. "Allison..." Meg stopped and turned to her office. She didn't need to explain herself. She looked on her desk and saw Allison had left her a card. Meg closed her eyes and took a deep breath. She realized she had been being unfair to Allison, and that Allison was the one person actually trying to help her. Meg walked back to the reception area. Allison was clearing off her desk.

"Can I start again?" Meg asked. Allison didn't look up and kept stacking papers together. "There's other stuff I never told you about in Granelle. It's just Jake...."

"You told me about Jake. You told me about Trevor," Allison said, sitting back down into her chair.

"I never told you what it felt like in that basement, the helplessness, the fears. I have never been so scared in my whole life." Meg sank down into the love seat near Allison's desk. "When I woke up on that bare dirty mattress, locked in this little room, I thought I was going to die. Knowing that Grant is out there somewhere has me scared. I feel helpless again."

"Then stay away from Granelle. You don't have to go back there and relive all that stuff. You've gotten really screwed up in your thinking. It's starting to screw everything else up in your life."

"It's not just Granelle. He could be here in Saratoga. Anywhere. I'm sorry I've been so hard on you, and I understand what you've been trying to do for me, Allison. But I've got to get Grant before he gets me."

"Do you hear yourself? He's not even after you. There is no proof that he's even back in the area."

"Proof. Now you sound like Reggie. I didn't need proof six years ago, and I was right then."

"I guess I can understand what you're going through, but you've got to get focused on your business again. Four of your clients are calling daily, and I'm stalling them all. How long do you think I can keep doing that before they start looking for another P.I.?"

"A few days ago, I saw Sam Craig on Broadway. He walked right by me and smiled."

"Sam? You mean the kid?"

"Only he's not a kid anymore. He smiled right at me." Meg got up and paced around the small room. "I tried to check it out and couldn't find out anything. No one I know in Granelle has seen Sam since he moved to Poughkeepsie years ago."

"Did you check Poughkeepsie?"

"I called the listing for Stanley Craig and got no answer. Nothing in the police system, and school's closed. Unless I go there, I can't get any other information."

"You don't think he has anything to do with Grant breaking out of jail, do you?"

"I don't know. Maybe they are still in contact, but I doubt it. But what are the chances of seeing Sam Craig, and then hearing that Trevor Grant breaks out of prison? What are the chances, Allison?"

"It's just a coincidence, and you're driving yourself crazy."

Meg stopped and shook her head. "It's not a coincidence. It's going to start again. Women are going to start disappearing again."

Allison stood up and went to her boss laying her hand on Meg's arm. "You are a logical person. Think about what you just said. First, how do you really know that was Sam Craig? It's been so many years since you've seen him. Second, even if Grant shows up in the area, you're no longer in Granelle. And if he does show up, the police are looking for him. Captain Bennett told me that the Saratoga Police have surveillance on your house. This isn't going to happen again."

"This didn't just happen. Somehow, it's all starting up again. And if Captain Bennett wants to bury his head in the sand...."

Allison interrupted her. "Meg, you're scaring me."

Meg looked hard at her. "Join the club. I'm terrified. This is starting again and I can't let Grant get me again. I'll kill him before he kills me. I swear to God, I will."

The coldness in Meg's voice sent a visible chill through Allison. "Meg...."

Meg pulled away. "I'm sorry for yelling at you. I need you to help me because I don't want to lose my business. But if you need to leave, I'll understand. I hated working for Reggie Bennett in the end, and if I've become him, I don't blame you for quitting."

Meg didn't wait for a response. She went into her office and closed the door. Looking out the big window, she watched people walking down Broadway. Sighing, she turned back to her desk. The light was flashing on her phone, and she pushed the button and listened to the messages that were left for her. She jotted a few things down on a pad and looked at some other notes.

Meg tapped her pen on the pad, and then she picked up the phone and called the number she had for Stanley Craig in Poughkeepsie. When the machine picked up again, she hung up. She dialed another number and waited. She dialed an extension.

When Meg got the voice mail, she left a message. "Look, I know that you have every right not to listen to me. It seems like I only turn to you when I have a problem. But once again, I need your help. I know you were told that Grant broke out of prison. I think that we need to talk. Please don't just ignore me. Call me when you can." Meg left her numbers and hung up again.

Meg sat staring at her computer when Allison knocked gently on her door. "Come on in," Meg said and looked up.

"I didn't get a chance to give you Captain Bennett's message."

Meg sighed, "Do I really care?"

Allison hesitated and then shrugged. "Probably not."

"He doesn't want me to help find Grant, right?"

"Yes, and he wanted you to know about the surveillance on your house."

"He just wants to let me know that he's in charge. Like I need that kind of reminder."

Allison nodded and then started closing the door. "Allison, can you get me the file on Mrs. Woods? Guess I'd better get back to making money."

Allison smiled at Meg and got the file for her. After Allison closed the office door, Meg put the file on the side and picked up the phone. She dialed the Craig's house again and hung up when the machine came on.

CHAPTER 14

The church was packed with people at the Wednesday night prayer meeting even though the service didn't start for a half an hour. Penny was bustling about, expressing her excitement about the number of people who packed their sanctuary to anyone who would listen. Jake had peeked through the little door that led from the offices to the sanctuary and recognized members of the press murmuring to each other. Although Jake knew he should be glad for the opportunity to share his beliefs about God with the media, he felt the service would turn into an impromptu press conference. In the crowd, he recognized many of the local townspeople who didn't attend his church either.

Jake sat at his desk holding his head in his hands, praying. He didn't want this night to turn into a circus, yet he knew there were faithful people in the church that had come to pray for Sarah and encourage him. There was a soft knock at his door. Jake looked up and wearily called out, "Come in."

The door opened and Pastor Walt stuck his head in the door. "Hear you could use a hand tonight," the older pastor said. Pastor Walt was in his sixties, but looked ten years younger.

Since retiring from actively pastoring the small church, Walt enjoyed long walks around town visiting everyone and was deeply tanned from these daily excursions. The gray streaks in his black wavy hair were the only thing that betrayed his age.

"Pastor Walt," Jake said. "How did you know I needed help?"

Walt walked up to the desk and sat down in front of it. "Penny called me and told me what was going on."

"She's something, isn't she?" Jake said with a weak smile. "I was just sitting here wondering how I was going to be able to go in there and face all those people."

"Seems like God has other plans. I'll surprise them all, parishioners and guests," Pastor Walt said with a little chuckle. "How are you holding up?"

"It's been tough. I want to spend every waking moment searching for

Sarah. I want to be involved in the investigation so I know everything the police know." Jake shook his head sadly. "But I know that it would only hurt the search. And now I've hurt my friendship with Reggie, and he won't let me near the station at all."

"We are all keeping Sarah in our prayers."

"I know, but I feel like it's getting too late," Jake's voice cracked.

"Until you know otherwise, don't give up hope. I should get to the sanctuary. We can talk afterwards."

Jake nodded as Pastor Walt stood and walked to the door, saying a silent prayer as he left. Jake was relieved that Pastor Walt had come and that he didn't have to face the people. He felt so lost, unsure of himself in the face of the unknown. His faith was shaken, and so was his ability to analytically put the pieces of the crime together. He only knew that his wife was missing and assumed taken by someone in Jake's past.

The office phone rang, pulling Jake from his thoughts. A light on his phone blinked and he waited until the answering machine at Penny's desk picked up the call. Jake listened, but the caller hung up. The phone started ringing again.

Figuring it must be an urgent caller, Jake picked up the line, "Granelle Gospel, may I help you?"

"Well, well, preacher. Been a long time." The voice chilled Jake.

"Where's my wife, Trevor?" Jake demanded.

Trevor laughed, "For right now, she's still alive. We need to talk about a few things."

"Oh?" Jake stood up.

"I suppose you've heard that I'm no longer in prison."

"Yes, Bennett told me."

"Good. Then you know that this is really me and that I have your wife."

"There has been no doubt in my mind that you had her."

"None at all? That's disappointing. I thought when you were running all over Saratoga looking for Doug that you had assumed he had taken her. Of course, you know better now."

"I followed the lead that the police had on Doug, but I believed it was you. I thought you might have gotten Doug to go along with you again."

Trevor laughed. "This is so much fun. How I've missed playing games with you, Detective."

"You know that I'm no longer a detective. I've been a pastor for a long time now."

"True enough. But you are at your best as a cop. Even now, you are probably trying to figure out where I am. You won't find me. I've played this game my entire life. I was only caught because of the mistakes that my old friend Shamus made. That won't happen again."

"Don't count on it."

"Oh, but I do. So, we are going to play a little game now. Since, as you reminded me, you are no longer a cop, I think you will cooperate with me and not tell our mutual friend, Reggie Bennett, about my call. You see, in all of the mistakes of the past, the biggest one was letting Shamus leave. I should never have let him leave. He betrayed me and the creatures. He walked away from his birthright and in the process, destroyed mine."

"What does this have to do with Sarah?"

"I'm getting to that. First, tell me how much you know about my escape."

"I'm not doing this with you. I'm going to hang up and call Bennett...."

"You hang up and I'll kill her." Trevor's voice conveyed a calm danger. When Jake said nothing, he continued. "We are going to do this my way. Tell me what I want to know."

"All I know is you got a letter, and a prison guard smuggled you out in the trunk of her car. After that, the police have told me nothing."

"Interesting. I'll give you the details so you know just how serious I am about what I'm expecting you to do. Shamus is dead. I lived for a long time with the belief that I was to take over as the keeper that I would inherit the birthright, the money, and the gifting. But Shamus stole that and has disowned me. He claims that the creature chose Sam over me. I know that it is up to the keeper to make that choice. So after destroying my life, Shamus hands over what is mine to that stupid child." As Trevor spoke he became more enraged. Jake was afraid to say anything, so he waited for Trevor to continue. Jake could hear Trevor breathing hard, trying to regain control.

Finally, he continued in a calmer voice, "I want that boy. I tried to find him, but can't. So, Mr. Detective, it's up to you. You find Sam Craig in exchange for your wife."

"You can't be serious."

"Oh, but I am. The only thing keeping your wife alive is the knowledge that the great detective, Jake Peterson, is going to find that kid and bring him to me."

"I have no idea where he is."

"Find him. I'll call you back soon. Be careful. Sarah's life is hanging on by just a thread."

Trevor hung up. Jake stood holding the receiver and finally sank back into his chair. Instinctively, Jake began to dial the police station but quickly hung up. Jake dialed his home number and waited for Doug to answer.

"Hello," Doug answered tentatively.

"This is Pastor Jake."

"Oh, is it okay that I answered your phone?"

"That's fine. I need you to go to my office and get a phone number."

"Your office? I haven't been in there before."

"That's okay. I have a yellow note on my desk with the number for Meg on it. I need the number."

"Okay, I'm heading up now. Is Meg...never mind," Doug muttered.

"You can ask me. Yes, she's the one who was my partner on the force. I need to ask her something about Sarah's disappearance. "

"Oh, aren't you preaching right now?"

Jake felt a stab of guilt and then shook it off. "No, Pastor Walt came and is doing the meeting. A lot of press showed up."

"There's two numbers here. Do you want both?"

"Just give me the one with the C next to it," Jake said, picking up a pen. He copied the number on a piece of scrap paper. "Thanks, Doug. I'll be back to the house as soon as I can. Is everything all right there?"

"Yep, me and Buddy are just sitting together watching those videos you left for me."

"Okay, I'll try not to be late. Make sure the house is locked up until I get back. I'm feeling really uncomfortable tonight."

"Sure, but we're fine. See you later," Doug hung up.

Jake quickly dialed the cell phone number Meg left on his voice mail. She picked up on the first ring. "Finally found time to call me back?" Meg's tone was sarcastic.

"Grant just called me," Jake said not taking her bait. "I need your help. I can't turn to Bennett or he's going to kill Sarah."

"What makes you think Grant is going to kill Sarah?"

"He took her. She's been missing for days."

"Took her? Bennett never told me she was missing."

"Can we meet, maybe at Joe's Steakhouse over here in Granelle?"

"I can be there in a half an hour."

"I'll be waiting." Jake hung up and walked out into the offices, leaving a note on Penny's desk saying he was gone for the night. He walked to his car and saw a few people outside talking. He recognized one of the reporters and ducked his head, hurrying toward his car. The last thing he wanted was for them to follow him to Joe's.

When Jake got to his car, he saw that he was blocked in, and any attempt to maneuver the car out of the church parking lot would draw the attention of the people milling around in front of the church. Jake walked past his car and up the side street next to the church. Walking up the block, he started to pray for strength before he talked to Meg. He hadn't talked to her in years, but there was no one else he could turn to, no one who would understand what he was feeling. Certainly she was the only person who knew exactly what Sarah was going through.

As Jake cut through a wooded area in back of someone's house, he stopped. How many times had Jake taken for granted the wooded isolation of Granelle? This place he had grown to love was just an isolated hideaway in the middle of the woods, a great place for a wild animal to hide or a perpetrator to commit crimes. For Sarah's sake, Jake forced himself to keep going.

Sam sat in the sanctuary of Granelle Gospel with the Mendozas, listening to the old preacher drone on and on. At least that's what it felt like to Sam. He couldn't understand why the Mendozas kept making him go to church. He didn't need church and his father never made him go anymore. He remembered both Pastor Walt and Pastor Jake.

Sam slouched down in the pew and wished he hadn't ever come to Granelle. His father had been right. He would never tell him that, but he was right. This trip brought back too many bad memories, Johnny had changed a lot, and he was stuck here for another two weeks. He had already tried to get his sister, Karen, to let him go to her apartment, but she said no. His Aunt Sheryl didn't want him at her place either. He knew it was his fault. He had been in a lot of trouble in Poughkeepsie. But right now, he wouldn't cause anyone trouble if he could just leave Granelle.

Sam glanced at his watch. He noticed he wasn't the only restless person in the congregation, as many had expected to see Pastor Jake tonight. But then, something Pastor Walt was saying caught his attention, and Sam sat up straight.

"...we need to pray that Sarah is found safe. Pastor Jake needs our prayers, too. How difficult it is for him to know his wife has been abducted. I understand the Stanwicks have gone to visit relatives out of state. This has been hard on Kathy, remembering how this happened to her in the past...."

Sam felt like he was suffocating. Missing! When the Mendozas talked about Mrs. Peterson, they never mentioned she was missing. Just like Mrs. Stanwick was before, just like himself. Sam had to get out of the church. He scooted past Mr. Mendoza, who got up and went with Sam outside. Out on the front lawn, Mr. Mendoza put his hand on Sam's shoulder.

"Sam, I should have told you about Mrs. Peterson. I'm sorry, but I thought it would be too difficult for you."

"Please tell me what happened," Sam choked out. He felt like he was being strangled and could hardly take a breath. Johnny came out and walked up to them.

"Pastor Jake came home the day before yesterday, and she was gone. They don't know where she is."

"What?" Sam gasped.

"Dad," Johnny said quietly, pointing toward the church where a small crowd was gathering. A few people had followed them to see what was going on.

"Come on, Sam. Let's just get you to the house. We can talk there." Mr. Mendoza took Sam's arm. Sam wanted to jerk away, but terror gripped him. He glanced over his shoulder and saw a few people heading their way.

The car had been parked on a side road because the church parking lot was full when they arrived. Mr. Mendoza let go of Sam and headed toward the driver's door while the two boys piled in the backseat. Once the car was moving Johnny asked, "What about Mom and Katie?"

"Text your mother and see if they can get a ride home with the Olsens. I don't want anyone to notice Sam."

"Can I smoke?" Sam asked, shaken.

"Just open the window." Johnny sent a text message to his mother while Sam fumbled with the window. His hands were shaking so badly, he could barely light the cigarette.

Fifteen minutes later, Mr. Mendoza, Sam, and Johnny were in the kitchen. Mr. Mendoza got everyone soda and sat down at the head of the table.

"Again, I'm sorry that you found out that way, Sam. I talked to your father about what was going on. We felt it was best to just keep it quiet. To be honest, I had hoped he would be home before you found out."

Sam felt calmer, and now he had to know everything. "It was Trevor, wasn't it." It was more a statement than a question.

"I don't know what's going on."

"Who else would want to take Pastor Jake's wife?" Sam asked. "The police actually think it was someone other than Trevor? Did you talk to Pastor Jake at all?"

"No. We haven't talked to Pastor Jake since you've been here."

"I saw the creature that night," Sam said quietly. "Do you remember when you caught me smoking outside?"

"I remember you smoking, but what creature, that wolf?"

"I know that the news just reported that it was some wolf that Trevor had, but it wasn't. It was some kind of a creature."

"You were a child..."

"It bit me," Sam said turning his hand over. The scar on his finger was long and white. "It changed me, somehow. I lived with that creature in the basement of the Hanson house for almost a week. It is no wolf."

"What does this have to do with anything?"

"Trevor told me then that if I told anyone about the creature, it would kill me. Somehow that creature chose me over Trevor. It wants me to be the keeper of it and its secrets."

"Sam, we don't believe in old myths."

"What I don't get is how Trevor is doing this. He's in jail. I was told he'd be there until he was a really old man. If the creature is back and a woman is missing, Trevor must be trying to reverse things. But, how can he?"

Sam looked at Mr. Mendoza for an answer. "Maybe I should at least let the police know you are staying here with us. Maybe that is best."

Johnny had been sitting silently, listening to everything. "Dad, wait for Mom to get home first. I have a bad feeling about this. I don't think Sam should mention the creature to the police either."

"Why?" Sam asked, turning to his friend.

"What if you are right about the creature and stuff? What happens to you if you start telling everyone about it? Maybe it will get you or my family. Or maybe it doesn't do anything, and that Trevor guy gets someone to get you."

"Boys, enough of this talk. I'll call the police and let them know you are here. Then we'll find out what we should do. Maybe it is better if you get out of Granelle, but let's let the police decide this. And I agree with Johnny, no talk about this creature."

CHAPTER 15

Joe's Steakhouse was the only restaurant in Granelle. There was a pizza place and a hamburger joint, but Joe's was the only place for steak or a sit-down meal. This late in the evening, most people in Granelle had already eaten. The bar was filled as Jake walked in, but the dining area was mostly deserted. Jake asked for a table in the back of the restaurant and told the waitress he was waiting for someone. He ordered coffee and sat, waiting for Meg.

Jake was surprised to see Meg show up ten minutes early. As she came over to the table, Jake couldn't help noticing how tired and stressed she looked.

"Hey," Meg said, sitting down across from Jake. Jake waited while the waitress took an order of coffee and dessert from Meg.

"You don't know how much I appreciate your coming here," Jake said quietly.

"Yeah, well, like I said in my message to you, I think we need each other to get through this. What is Bennett's problem?"

"I don't know. He told me a few things. But he's really mad at me now. I talked to Doug Angelos after Reggie told me he was a suspect."

"Angelos? He's in town?"

"Yes, he came for track season."

"Just another coincidence? Too many of them keep popping up. What made you go talk to him after Bennett told you he was a suspect?"

"Doug came to see me just before Sarah disappeared. I needed to know from him if he had anything to do with this."

"Did he?"

"No, he was facing his own personal demons. But now, he's accepted the Lord and living at my house right now."

"Are you crazy? How can you let him stay with you?"

"I'm considering some alternatives. But he needs to get away from the environment and have a chance to learn how to live as a Christian."

"I don't understand you. Religion really changed you into a different person. The Jake that I knew wouldn't let an ex-con live with him."

"I know you don't understand, but I'm not the old Jake that you knew. I really am a changed person."

"Well, I guess I have to give you some credit for wanting to help that guy. But let's get back to Sarah. I can't believe that Bennett didn't tell me. I have half a mind to go tell him off." Meg was beginning to raise her voice, and Jake put a restraining hand on her arm.

"I know you're really mad. But I need you to stay cool about this. Grant has Sarah and he will kill her unless I get him what he wants."

Meg narrowed her eyes at him. "And what's that? Me? Did you lure me here...?"

"No!" Jake shook his head and pulled his hand back. "Sam. He wants Sam."

"Sam?" Meg took a deep breath. Before she could continue, the waitress came with her coffee and apple pie. Meg waited until she left. "I saw Sam in Saratoga."

Jake was surprised. "I was hoping you would help me track him down in Poughkeepsie."

"Why? You aren't seriously going to turn Sam over to Grant, are you?"

"No...I don't know. I'm scared for Sarah. I love her so much and don't want to see Grant hurt her."

Meg just nodded and didn't respond. To hear Jake say he loved Sarah hurt her. She wanted to just get up and leave, but she knew that she needed Jake's help as much as he needed hers. There was no one else she could trust to help her nail Grant. The fact that his wife was missing might actually motivate him to really be involved in helping her. Not like before, when he fought every lead she had.

"Okay," Meg said. "I think we need to tell each other everything that we know. I didn't tell Bennett about Sam, but he never told me about Sarah either. Let's combine our information and see what we have."

"Sounds like a good idea," Jake said smiling weakly. "To be honest, I'm feeling...."

"And that's another thing. I don't want to know what you're feeling. I know it's been a lot of years since there was anything between us. You want honesty?" Meg stopped and looked into Jake's blue eyes. She plunged ahead. "I still have a thing for you. It hurt me a lot when you married Sarah. There I said it. Can you still work with me?"

"Meg, I never knew you still felt that way. It's been over five years since you moved to Saratoga. I don't know what to say...."

"You moved on. This is my problem."

"Meg, I thought for a long time about you and wanting a life with you. But when I went into the ministry, there just didn't seem a way with us having such opposing beliefs. Then Sarah moved to Granelle."

"I get it, Jake. But I can put all that aside for now if you can. Will it be too weird that I'm helping you find your wife?"

Jake looked at her hard and then shook his head. "You're the only one I trust. You were always good at investigating."

"Bottom line. For me this isn't about finding Sarah. This is about getting Grant."

"I get it, Meg," Jake said. He motioned to the waitress and asked for more coffee. After she left, they sat for over an hour talking about Grant, Reggie, Sam, and how they were going to get Sarah back alive.

Mr. Mendoza answered the door about an hour later. He brought Reggie to the kitchen where his wife was waiting. Sam was outside smoking and talking to Johnny.

"Please sit down. We have some things we need to tell you," Mr. Mendoza said, offering a chair.

"The dispatcher said you might have information on Mrs. Peterson," Reggie started. "But this better be important. Otherwise, you should have come to the station in the morning."

"We feel it is. Actually, let me get the boys." Mr. Mendoza got up and called the boys in from outside. Reggie frowned as the two teens walked in. Sam hesitated, staring at Reggie. There was a look of fear in his eyes. "Johnny, go wait upstairs while we talk to the officer."

Johnny left the room but sat halfway down the stairs, listening. Reggie watched as Sam took a seat at the table. "These folks think you have something very important to tell me about the Peterson case."

Sam swallowed and glanced at Mr. Mendoza. He nodded and reassured Sam. "It's okay, son. He needs to know."

"What do I need to know?" Reggie asked gruffly. "You see something that day?"

"You're a detective?" Sam stared at Reggie.

"I'm the captain. I'm the boss of the detectives."

"Do you remember me?"

Reggie continued to frown. "Look kid, you have something to tell me or not?"

"I remember you. You don't look as big as I remember though."

Reggie started to get up. "I don't appreciate coming out...."

"Captain Bennett, this is Sam Craig," Mr. Mendoza said interrupting.

Reggie settled back in the chair, with a look of disbelief as he saw that it was Sam sitting across from him. "Sam Craig, the boy. What are you doing here?" Reggie asked.

Sam was put off by Reggie and just shrugged. Mr. Mendoza spoke up for Sam. "He is here visiting our family."

"How long has he been here?"

"About two weeks, a little more than two weeks."

Reggie cleared his throat. "What made you decide to call and let me know he was here tonight?"

"Sam just found out tonight that Mrs. Peterson is missing," Mr. Mendoza began. "When he found out he was very distraught. We felt it best to notify you that he was here in case there is a connection to the past incidents."

"What do you think, Sam? Is this about the past?" Reggie looked directly at Sam. When Mr. Mendoza started to talk, Reggie stopped him. "No, I want to hear this from Sam."

"I don't know," Sam finally said, looking away from Reggie's glare.

"You can either start talking to me now or I can take you down to the station."

Sam looked back at Reggie. "Why?"

"Let's just say you're a suspect. You have ties to the Petersons, you just happen to be in Granelle when she disappears..."

"You think I did this?"

"You're as good a suspect as anyone else," Reggie said, leaning into the table. "Now what do you know about this case?"

"Nothing." Sam was defiant at Reggie's attitude.

"Please, Captain Bennett. Sam has not been alone since he got to our house. The boys have mostly been hanging around the house, and they have always been together. My son can tell you that," Mr. Mendoza said.

Reggie went on, disregarding Mr. Mendoza. "I've already been checking up on you. Your school record is pretty bad. Fighting, truancy, reprimands, not a pretty picture. Even found out that the school considered filing a PINS petition on you. Did you know that?"

"What's that?" Sam glared back at Reggie.

"A 'person in need of supervision.' Seems the school doesn't think your father is doing a good job of parenting."

"Leave my father out of this."

"Speaking of your father, where is he? I don't see him sitting at this table. Isn't he concerned about you?"

Sam got up and shoved the chair against the table. Pointing a finger at Reggie, he shouted, "You don't know anything about me or my life."

Reggie got up too and starting reaching for his handcuffs. "Maybe I'll do your school a favor."

Mr. Mendoza stepped between them. "This is no way to handle this, Captain Bennett. Don't you realize how difficult it has been on the Craigs since they left Granelle?"

"You're going to tell me how I should do my job, Mr. Mendoza?" Reggie didn't take his eyes off Sam.

"Of course not. But my friend Mayor Thompson might. I asked you to come here because I was concerned for a boy whose father left him in my care. We are concerned about him because the last time people went missing in Granelle, one of them was Sam. If you want to accuse this boy of something, you can do so at my lawyer's office in the morning. Until then, I think it best you leave."

At the mention of the mayor, Reggie seemed to calm a little. "As I said when I arrived, we should have just handled this down at the station in the morning."

"Perhaps, but that's not going to happen now."

"I still need to question Sam," Reggie said.

Mr. Mendoza stood next to Sam. "This boy needs no more trauma in his life. I will confer with my attorney as to the best way to handle this. I am very disappointed that you come into my house when I'm the one that called you and you treat Sam like this. And we find out that you were already investigating him. What reason would you have to look at his school record?"

"Anyone tied to Grant is being contacted. We wanted to be sure that Sam's family knew of the escape."

"That's not a reason to check into his school records. There are confidentiality laws that you have probably violated. I think we're done here. You can leave now."

"Fine," Reggie turned to leave.

"Wait," Sam said. Reggie turned back, looking like he was about to explode. Sam began to tremble with nerves. He licked his lips and stammered. "I... I saw the creature."

"I don't think that's helpful," Mr. Mendoza said.

Johnny came up behind Reggie, shaking his head no.

"I was outside having a cigarette. It was in the backyard."

"What does this have to do with Mrs. Peterson?" Reggie asked.

"I don't know. I'm just scared," Sam practically whispered. "I'm scared."

Mr. Mendoza put his arm around Sam's shoulders and murmured something to him that Reggie couldn't hear. Sam nodded and waited to see what Reggie would say.

Reggie shrugged, "There's no way that could be the same animal."

"I know it is. I was locked in a basement with it for a week. I know that creature."

"Apparently there *are* some things that we need to discuss. Can we sit?" Reggie said, gesturing towards the table. Mr. Mendoza nodded as Johnny walked into the kitchen. His mother tried to stop him, but he pushed passed her and sat down next to Sam.

"You think you have something to add, young man?" Reggie asked Johnny as he sat down.

"Probably not. But the next time you accuse my best friend of something, I want to be sitting right here," Johnny said. Sam turned to Johnny with a look of surprise.

"Fine," Reggie sighed. "Jake Peterson was one of my best detectives and is a close friend. I'll admit that I'm being hard on everyone, not just you. To have the past come back like this and have it hit the Petersons...."

"How do you think I feel?" Sam said softly. "Trevor was going to kill me. He had already killed Mom."

"I know that," Reggie said. "It just shocked me when you walked in. With all the stuff going on in Granelle, I didn't really need another surprise. You aren't the only one that claims to have seen the animal in recent days. "

"Who else saw it?" Sam asked.

"Sarah Peterson saw it a few days before she disappeared. And there's another thing you need to know. Trevor Grant broke out of prison around the same time. I've contacted all the other victims. Obviously with you here, I had no way of contacting you. The police in Poughkeepsie have been keeping surveillance on your house."

"Trevor's got Mrs. Peterson," Sam said.

"Well, we don't know that for sure. There is another suspect."

"I know for sure," Sam said. "There's no one else that would do this. It's because of the creature. You've got to stop him. He wants to do that ritual thing to make him the keeper. He's going to keep going until he has the four and me. It takes four women to complete the ritual, and knowing Trevor, he will want revenge, too."

"Has he been in contact with you?" Reggie asked.

"You're kidding, right?"

Reggie shook his head. Sam went on. "No, he hasn't. But how does he know I'm in Granelle again? Why now?"

"*Does* he know you're in Granelle?" Reggie asked.

"Why else would this be happening?"

"I don't know yet. But, I intend to find out."

CHAPTER 16

Jake had arrived back at the house late. He quietly came in the back door and stood listening to the television in the living room. He found Doug and Buddy sleeping on the couch. Buddy opened his eyes and wagged his tail at Jake. Doug never moved, so Jake shut off the television and went upstairs to the bedroom. He found Felix curled up on Sarah's pillow. Jake sat on the bed and picked up the cat. He stretched in Jake's arms and started to purr.

Jake lay down on the bed, holding Sarah's cat. "I promise I'll do everything I can to get her back," Jake told Felix. The feline settled against his chest and soon was back to sleep. Jake replayed the past few hours and wondered if he was making a mistake not talking this out with Reggie.

Jake started to pray about the situation and was soon asleep.

Morning light poured in the window as Jake stretched. He heard Doug moving around downstairs and groaned. He got up and took a hot shower. The smell of the fresh coffee hit him as he headed down the stairs.

"Got in late last night?"

"Yeah, I got hung up," Jake poured himself a cup of coffee. Buddy came up behind Jake and pawed at him. Jake petted Buddy on the head as he sat down at the table.

"We need to have a talk, Doug," Jake began. Doug looked up from one of Jake's Bibles with expectancy. "The last thing I want to do is put you in jeopardy. I think having you stay here isn't the best for you right now."

"I'm trying not to be in the way," Doug said, closing the book.

"You're not in the way. In fact, I'm enjoying having your company, and so does Buddy. You have been such a big help and support, but staying here is going to endanger your life."

"I know that Trevor is out there, but I'm being careful."

"I'm going to tell you something that only one other person knows. I trust this will stay between us."

"Sure, who would I tell anyway?"

"Trevor called me at the church last night. He has Sarah and is ready to kill her if I don't meet certain demands. I'm not going to tell you what those demands are, but he already knew I had tracked you down to Saratoga, so he is close enough to be watching."

"Maybe I can help you with that."

"No," Jake shook his head. "I need to get my focus back into investigating. I can't do that and be worried that Trevor is going to snatch you. I have an alternative for you, though. One that I think will be a great opportunity."

"Okay..." he replied. "But I don't see why I can't stay and help you. You saved my life; I owe you that."

"What I'm asking you for is simple. Remember anything you can now about Grant, and then we will get you to safety. Think about Grant. Any places he might be hiding. My old partner is coming by soon, and she's going to ask you all kinds of questions. The questions might be hard, but know that neither one of us believes you have anything to do with Sarah's disappearance. We just need to know everything we can so we can track down Grant."

"Okay," Doug scowled. "But I already told you everything I know."

"I'm sure you have. But I've been so upset, I don't think I remember half of what you told me. That's why I want you to talk to my old partner."

"That's Meg, right?

"Do you remember her?"

"Sure do. She was with you that day you arrested me."

Jake nodded and then went on. "Anyway, I really want to get you out of town today after you talk to Meg. I've been considering this for a couple of days now. I have a friend who is a pastor in New Rochelle. He runs a halfway house there. I already talked to him about you and your situation, and he'd like you to come and work at the house in exchange for room and board."

"I don't know about this."

"There are a lot of chances for you there. My friend said he will help you learn more about the Bible. They have nightly meetings you can attend and get to meet other Christians. Plus, you will be close enough to Granelle that we can still get together."

"You've already decided, haven't you?" Doug was despondent.

"It's a great ministry where you can help and learn too. It is ultimately your decision, but you've trusted me before. Please trust me again. I have your best interest in mind. You think about it. I want to go outside, sit with my coffee, and pray."

Doug nodded and turned back to the old Bible. Jake took Buddy outside with him and let the big dog run around in the back yard. Jake sat in a lawn chair and watched Buddy throw a ball up in the air and chase it. After a few minutes, Jake heard a car pull up in the driveway and went to the side of the house to see who it was. Buddy ran up to the car, wagging his tail and jumping around.

Jake watched as Reggie opened the door and petted the excited Buddy. Reggie looked up to see Jake standing at the back corner of the house. He pushed Buddy to the side and stood up. Buddy ran back to get the ball and dropped it at Reggie's feet.

Reggie ignored the ball and walked up to Jake. "I hope it's okay that I dropped by."

"Sure," Jake said. "I'm just sitting outside praying and thinking."

"Can I join you for a bit?" Jake shrugged and went back to the chair. Reggie sat next to him, squeezing into the tight lawn chair. They sat in silence for a few long moments. Jake began to wonder if the church phone was bugged and Reggie knew about the call from Trevor. For now, Jake wasn't going to say anything. He wanted Sarah back alive.

"Got any more of that?" Reggie pointed at the coffee cup.

"In the kitchen. But so is Doug," Jake said, taking a drink from his cup.

Reggie made a disgusted sound and went back to silence. Jake watched as Buddy sniffed around near the woods. Buddy's tail dropped and hair began to stand up on his back. Jake set the cup on the ground and walked toward the dog.

"Buddy, what'd you find?" Jake neared the dog and put his hand on Buddy. The dog whimpered. Jake scanned the woods and saw nothing. But there was an oddly familiar musky scent.

"What is it, Peterson?" Reggie came up behind Jake.

"An animal left a scent here that's bothering Buddy. I can actually smell it too. Really strong. Oddly familiar."

Jake stepped into the woods. He looked around and noticed large animal footprints near a tree. Buddy ran back to the house. Jake turned back to Reggie. "Recognize these?"

Reggie came up to the tree and knelt down next to the prints. "They look like those tracks from that wolf."

"Sarah was right. He's been here."

"Again, you mean," Reggie said, as he stood and looked around in the woods. "Those tracks are fresh. The scent wouldn't be this strong either."

Jake saw a few more tracks and followed them to where they got lost in the deep vegetation. He walked back to the tree and looked up at his house. He wondered if that creature had been sitting there watching when he got home last night.

Reggie broke the silence. "I came because there are questions I should ask you. As much as I hate it, I have questions for Angelos, too. I'm still mad that you went behind my back like you did."

"We told you everything that we knew."

"You both told me what you thought I should know. But I have other questions."

Jake looked at Reggie, surprised. "Why? Has something changed?"

"No, not really."

"I don't understand."

"I haven't personally handled a case since I came to Granelle. But I chose to handle this one because of you. I find I'm not being objective. I'm mad that it's Sarah and you. I'm just plain mad. So, I stormed out of here and now realize that I didn't have enough detailed information about what really happened with Angelos. And since he was involved with Grant before, maybe there is something he remembers that can help the case."

"Will you let me help?"

"No, she's still your wife."

"Okay. You should know that I'm setting Doug up in a halfway house downstate."

Reggie took a deep breath and waited a moment before answering. "That's not a good idea. I still think he's involved."

"He's not. I've spent a lot of time with him. He needs to get out of the area before he becomes a target. He will still be accessible through me, but I don't want anyone to know where I'm putting him."

"That's not really your call, Jake," Reggie said tersely.

"Thought we just came to an understanding, Reggie." Jake headed out of the woods. "This is already the second time I'm saying this today: trust me. Doug needs to get away. I need him to get away, too. But I'll know where he is."

"I want to talk to him before he leaves," Reggie said, walking with Jake back to the house.

"Sure. Like I said, he's in the kitchen. But go easy on him if you want him to open up."

"You expect me to go easy on a suspect?" Reggie sputtered.

"Not really, but try to be nice." Jake sat back down in the lawn chair.

"You aren't going in with me?"

"You're the investigator in the case. Go ask your questions," Jake said. "But I'll guarantee you that nothing he says will help you find Sarah."

Jake picked up his coffee cup. It was lukewarm now, but he still took a drink and then called Buddy over. He heard the door slam shut behind him and prayed for Doug and Reggie.

CHAPTER 17

Trevor felt trapped and restless in the small empty house and needed to get out. The woman had just been given a large dose of drugs, but he still went into the small bedroom and tied her to the bed frame. He needed to get outside and check things out in town. Trevor got in the stolen car and drove toward Granelle. He knew he needed to be careful, so he took back roads toward the isolated part of the town, near the old house that he had rented the last time. This was the part of town that Trevor knew very well.

The woods were dense and there were very few houses. Trevor was able to pull the car right into an old path in the woods. The light colored car was easy enough to hide from the road. Trevor really didn't expect that anyone would come back and see the car anyway.

It was muggy and hot. Dark clouds overhead threatened rain, but that didn't bother Trevor. The freedom of the woods was a relief after being in prison and now the cramped old house he was hiding in. How he longed to just be able to live in the woods, away from everything and everyone. Once he got the money, he just might live in isolation from the outside world, at least for a while.

Trevor knew that people were probably still out searching for Sarah. But he knew how to skirt around people in the woods. He had learned those lessons as a child. Deep in the woods, there were caves that had served Trevor's purposes in the past. He headed toward them, hoping that he would find some of the old possessions that would help him now. He wondered what the police did with the belongings that he had left at the Hanson house when he was arrested. Maybe there, too, he could find some items that he could use.

It took Trevor a long time to walk to the caves. He stayed in the woods looking at the rock face, making sure no one was there. Finally, he quickly went to the large cave where he had held his victims in the past. It took a few moments for his eyes to adjust to the darkness inside the rock mountain. The coolness of the cave felt good to Trevor after the hike in the hot woods.

On a rock ledge, Trevor found some things he had left long ago. The old tools, ropes, and keys looked untouched since they were last used. Trevor wondered if anyone even knew he had used the caves before. Of course, Sam did. Trevor went in deeper.

This cave was connected to a few smaller ones by tunnels hollowed into the rock. Trevor knew that deeper still he had some other things hidden. It was pitch black this far away from the entrance, but Trevor knew where he was going. Just trailing his hand along the stone wall, he knew which turns to take to get deeper into the mountain. As he entered the deepest cave, a deep growling stopped him.

"Is it you?" Trevor asked into the darkness. At the sound of his voice, the growling stopped. "It is you. Have you been waiting all this time for me?"

Trevor advanced into the cave. He was unsettled by the silence. He still remembered the last encounter he had with the creature. The last time the creature had attacked him at Sam's command. But Sam wasn't here right now. The creature knew Trevor and knew that he could take care of it.

"I was in prison. But I heard that Shamus has died. I came here to fulfill my duties to you and to the legacy."

Trevor felt around on a ledge until he felt an old lantern. If he was right, there would be matches nearby to light it. His hand fell on the matches and he quickly struck a match on the stone. As he lit the lantern, the cave quickly filled with light. Trevor turned to see the creature lying on an old filthy blanket on the floor.

"So, last I remember, you didn't want me as the keeper. Has that changed? There is no one else who knows about your needs and has the ability to care for you. I am here now. Will you accept me now?"

The creature sat up and stared at Trevor. Its eyes glowed red in the dim light of the lantern. Trevor approached it, and it just sat waiting. The creature narrowed its eyes as Trevor dropped to his knees and reached out his hand. It moved back away from Trevor.

"I know you are angry at me for what happened before. But it was as much Shamus's fault as mine. He wanted that boy, and I knew he was wrong for you. Because of that, you were left alone. I'm sorry for that. But I could not come. I was in prison and just got out. I'm here now, and I will take you back to France. We can start all over again and find a new boy."

The creature was still and alert. Its fur stood up on the back of its neck and it growled. Trevor tried again to reach out to the creature, but it got up and moved away from him. Trevor felt himself getting angry, but knew it would do him no good to be angry at the creature. He knelt on the hard stone floor and watched the creature. In order for Trevor's plan to work, the creature had to accept him.

There was something about the creature that only those with the knowledge understand. Because he had almost become the keeper, Trevor knew the creature's secrets. The myth that the creature was the offspring from the breeding of a wolf with the werewolf was true. But true knowledge of the creatures went beyond the myth: that original werewolf had great evil power that was passed to his descendents, together with a great fortune.

Irish legends and folklore all carry some element of truth. The keeper's folklore held deep fear for those in that Irish countryside where the myth originated. For they knew the werewolf, and he was a man feared and hated. But when he was captured and later killed, the townspeople were shocked to hear about the offspring that they referred to as creatures. Those dark creatures held the form of their wolf ancestors, but also the evil and intelligence of their human descendants. It was those traits that caused the keepers to do evil deeds and rituals demanded by the werewolf for them to inherit his vast financial fortune. Shamus was the last Irish descendant from that original town to keep the creatures' secrets and do the necessary rituals to keep the legacy alive.

Trevor stood up and looked around the cave. It was time for him to relocate to Granelle. He found an old collapsible cage that he had used before. He could easily move it to the big cave and bring Sarah back from town. It would be risky, but he could control the situation much better from here than over at Lake Desolation. Here he would be able to keep an eye on his old friend, Jake Peterson.

Trevor turned back to the creature. "I'm going to make this up to you. You will see that I am worthy to be the keeper. I have a plan. Just wait and see what I'm going to do."

The creature continued to watch Trevor as he set up the cage. Trevor found an old padlock and tested the keys. The rust was thick, and the key barely turned in the lock. He set it to the side and continued to make preparations to bring Sarah to the cave. There were other things he would need to complete the rituals, but Trevor believed those items were at the old house unless the police had taken them. He knew he would need to go out there, but first he needed to get everything set up here.

The creature laid down on the dirty blanket again. It would watch and see what Trevor was up to. But it knew that in one of the houses, the boy he wanted was waiting to do his bidding too.

CHAPTER 18

Meg was frustrated when she saw Reggie's car at Jake's house. She had hoped to get working early, but knew she couldn't go in until Reggie left. She went back to town and got coffee, drove around the neighborhood a couple times, then sat waiting around a bend until he finally left.

Meg was surprised at the change in Doug. This wasn't the same incoherent, insane man that she helped Jake arrest. Doug was joking with Jake when Meg came to the kitchen door. They made small talk while Doug cleaned up the few cups and made fresh coffee for all of them. When Meg started asking Doug questions, Jake excused himself and went upstairs to his office.

Jake sat at his desk and saw one of his Bibles on the side. He hadn't read his Bible since the night Sarah disappeared, which was unusual for him. Jake opened the Bible and began to read from the Gospel of Luke. As if reading for the first time, Jake felt awestruck by how Jesus prayed when he went through His darkest hour, just before being betrayed by Judas. Jake read, "And being in an agony [of mind], He prayed [all the] more earnestly and intently, and His sweat became like great clots of blood dropping down upon the ground."

In his own dark hour, Jake had found it difficult to pray; he was at a loss for words. But with the realization that Jesus' response was to pray more earnestly and intently, Jake pushed his chair out of the way and got on his knees. The agony in Jake's heart caused him to cry out to God in despair for Sarah's protection and deliverance. He begged God to keep their baby safe and to give him and Meg the ability to track down Trevor. He prayed on and on for the first time in days, pouring his heart out.

Meg found Jake still on his knees next to his desk when she was done questioning Doug. She watched him for a while, trying to understand this man. She wondered how he could maintain faith in God when his wife was being held by Trevor. Meg never held onto any religion. As a child, her parents took her to Sunday school, but by her teen years, church held no interest for her. Jake's sudden conversion and passion for Christ while they were engaged turned her off. She blamed his faith for their breakup, and Meg didn't want anything to do with church, God, or faith of any kind, whether it was Christian or any other religion. The very religious faith that Jake held to, Meg perceived as a weakness.

Last night at the steakhouse, Meg saw a glimpse of a new Jake. Sure it had been five years since she talked to him, but those years had totally changed him. Maybe it was because he was a minister, but Jake was so concerned with not doing the wrong thing that Meg was sure this was going to hamper his ability to really assist in the investigation.

But what struck Meg most as she watched Jake pray was that she didn't love him anymore. She pulled the door closed and stood in the hall for a moment as she let that realization wash over her. She smiled to herself as she went back downstairs.

It was a half an hour later when Jake got off his knees. He finally felt ready to face whatever was going to happen. He sat back at his desk and picked up the phone, calling the church.

"Penny, this is Pastor Jake," he said when she answered. "Is Keith in yet?"

"Yes, he got in a while ago. Are you coming in today?"

"No, that's why I'm calling. I need a few days off. I want to talk to Keith about doing the Sunday service. I thought maybe you could call Pastor Walt and see if he can help out with counseling and some of the office work."

"Sure, I'll take care of that," Penny replied. Pastor Jake, I'm praying for you." Penny then put his call through to Keith.

"Hey, Keith, how'd it go with the youth last night?" Jake asked when Keith answered. Keith was the new associate pastor for Granelle Gospel. Keith looked young enough to be one of the teens that Keith enjoyed leading, and his on fire faith and charisma was infectious with the youth. Keith and a group of the teens had taken their passion for God to the streets of Saratoga last night, trying to reach the community for Christ.

"It was awesome!" Keith's excitement could hardly be contained even on the phone. "We talked to this group of kids. I think they are serious about coming to our end-of-the-summer retreat!"

"Think you can bottle some of your enthusiasm for a message on Sunday?" Jake knew Keith would jump at the chance to preach.

"I'd love it!"

Jake smiled as he talked to Keith. With the church in good hands, Jake was ready to get to work helping Meg. Jake hung up, thankful for the church staff that would fill in for him. He knew that each person would go above and beyond to make sure that Jake didn't worry about the church. He then called Walt and got his answering machine, so he left a message explaining his need for a few days' leave. As he got off the phone, Meg knocked on the office door.

"Sorry to bother you, but I'm through talking to Doug. I know you wanted to leave for New Rochelle when I was done."

"I'm ready. I've decided to take a few days off from the church so we can work together. If you can't take the time off right now...."

"You're kidding, right?" Meg said. "I've hardly worked in the past few days."

"That's not good, Meg. You can't lose business."

"I'd rather lose a little business than my life. It's more important that we get Grant."

"I need to show you something outside. I'm just going to get my camera first. Give me a few minutes, I'll be right down."

Jake went to the bedroom as Meg went back downstairs. Doug was busy playing with the cat on the floor. Meg stood on the bottom step watching the big man pull a string for the cat to chase. Buddy lay next to Doug with his head on his leg, watching Felix jumping around after the string. Doug clearly was enjoying playing with the cat.

"Have you always been good with animals?" Meg asked from the steps. Doug looked up at her and then nodded shyly. "It's nothing you should be ashamed of. The animals just seem to love you."

"Yeah, most anyway," Doug continued playing with Felix.

Meg walked into the room and sat on the couch. "Most? That implies that some don't."

"That animal Trevor had didn't like me."

"I don't think that animal likes too many people."

"Why do you think that is? Someone was mean to it, so it's mean to people?"

"I'm not much of an animal person. But I think it's got to be a lot like people. Some people are mean because they were treated badly, but some are just bad."

"Like Trevor?"

"For a while, I felt bad for Trevor. But I think he was one of those people that was born bad."

"I don't believe that," Jake said, coming down the stairs. "I think that he was turned bad by his circumstances."

"You can defend him after what he's done?" Meg asked.

"I believe that there is hope for anyone to be changed."

"We don't know how many women he's killed. He tormented us in that basement and now he has Sarah...."

"I know all that. But I also know that the apostle Paul said he was the chief of sinners, yet his life was changed." Meg stood up to confront Jake, but he stopped her. "We won't agree on this, and I don't want to argue with you. We need to stay unified to do what we need to do."

"I know that religion can change people," Meg conceded. "I see you and how it changed you. But someone like Grant?"

"Meg, you know that Grant was abducted by O'Leary when he was a child and forced into this life. That's why I believe he was turned by his circumstances."

"Okay, but do you honestly believe that your religion can change him?"

"We've had this conversation before. This isn't just a religion that I do on Sundays. My faith is in a personal relationship with God, something that transforms my life on a daily basis. That type of faith is life changing, transforming, and yes, it can even change someone like Grant."

"Well, I don't believe that."

"I know you don't. So, why don't I show you what I found? It's something Buddy discovered this morning," Jake said going toward the kitchen. Meg stood there with her arms crossed and then sighed. She looked down at Doug, who was still playing with the cat, and then followed Jake.

Meg found Jake already crossing the backyard to the woods. She ran to catch up with him. "Hey, can you wait for me?" she asked.

"Sorry, I'm just getting a little anxious about getting on the road. This morning, Buddy was out here with me and he got really freaked out by the woods. When I got over here, I could smell this really bad odor. Right here," Jake stopped just outside the wood line. "Smell it?"

"Yes, it smells like that creature," Meg said with a shudder.

"Now look here," Jake stepped into the woods near the tree. He pointed to the ground and showed Meg the prints. Meg followed the tracks like Jake did until they weren't visible. Jake took a couple of pictures of the prints to see if they could find something similar on the Internet when they got back. Meg looked all around until she picked up the trail again.

"I really need to get going with Doug," Jake finally said.

"Okay, I'll talk to you later," Meg was distracted, looking around at the ground for more tracks.

"Meg, I got a really bad feeling about you being in the woods alone."

"The trail is fresh, though," she said, walking back toward Jake.

"All the more reason for you to stay out of the woods."

"We should track it. If we find that animal, we might find Trevor and Sarah."

"That's a big maybe for you to take the risk of running into the creature alone."

"Let me get my gun and let's go," Meg stepped out of the woods.

"I need to get Doug out of town. Besides, Reggie says it doesn't look like Trevor's in Granelle."

Meg sighed. "This is frustrating. I just want to do something."

"So do I. But the creature's been here before, and I'm sure he's still watching me. We can follow it another time...together."

"Okay," Meg said, knowing that as soon as she could she was going to follow that trail. They walked back to the house together.

Jake called his friend and made arrangements to drive Doug halfway to New Rochelle. His friend would meet them at one of the rest areas on the thru-way. Jake left Meg with the camera so she could download the pictures on his computer and look for information online. Jake told her not to go into the woods without him. He didn't really want to leave; rather, he wanted to start working right away with Meg. But he felt he owed it to Doug to keep him safe from Trevor and in a place where he could get help and healing from years of mental anguish.

Not wanting to outright lie to Jake, Meg spent an hour searching the Internet for some information on the Craig family. She finally stumbled onto a notice of Stanley's engagement, with a July wedding planned. Now she just had to find out where the wedding had taken place and see if anyone knew where the Craigs would have gone on their honeymoon.

Meg couldn't sit still any longer. She went to her car and pulled a gun out of the trunk, making sure it was loaded. She put it in the waistband of her jeans and stuck an extra clip in her pocket. She went back to the woods and found the tracks again. By now, the day had turned hot. The August sun was blocked by the trees, but the humidity was unbearable. However, Meg was determined to hunt that creature down and kill it. She refused to let anything stop her this time, not stifling heat, not fear, not the police, not even Jake.

The creature's prints led her to the old railroad tracks and ended. Meg scanned both sides of the rails and could not pick up the trail. Gnats flew around her head annoying her, and her jeans stuck to her legs, but she pressed on. Hours later, hot, sweating, and dehydrated, Meg had only one place left to look, the old Hanson place, the place that still haunted Meg's worst nightmares.

Meg walked down the railroad bed toward the desolate section of Granelle. She knew the paths that crisscrossed the tracks led to a few houses, but the path she needed was the farthest away. When she finally reached the entrance, deep shadows filled the woods. Meg pulled her revolver out and cocked the trigger. Holding the gun in her right hand, she took a deep breath and followed the path.

The woods were thicker and denser than Meg remembered, but she pushed through. The undergrowth pulled at her and the path was hardly discernable. Finally she stood staring at the back of the old Hanson house. She had a feeling of being watched as she stepped out of the woods into the overgrown backyard. The backyard was being taken over by weeds and vegetation, as the house had been sitting vacant for so many years. She glanced around the yard and then back to the house. Nothing moved.

Old police tape, aged and faded, still blocked off the backdoor. Meg walked up the dilapidated back porch, and a board protested under her feet. She tried to see into the kitchen windows, but grime made it impossible. She walked around the house and saw that it was deserted. She looked into the broken windows and saw the thick dust and dirt that accumulated over years of neglect.

Meg put her gun away and headed toward the road. Feeling miserable and hot, Meg started the long walk back to Jake's house on the other end of town. The dead end road led her past the Craigs' old house, and Meg barely glanced at it. Crisscrossing roads, passing houses, Meg let her thoughts drift back over the clues she knew. As she passed the Mendoza house, she didn't see the two teen boys sitting in the tree house smoking.

CHAPTER 19

Sam saw Meg and watched as she disappeared down the street. The dark shadow that had been watching Sam saw her too. It looked up at Sam and then quietly followed her, staying deep in the shadows.

"Hey, that's that woman cop," Johnny said when he saw Meg pass. "Think she's looking for Mrs. Peterson?"

"I don't think so," Sam said as he flicked his cigarette toward the woods. "She's probably just taking a walk. The police have been organizing search groups from the church."

"Didn't think about that," Johnny said. "Hey, why don't we see about renting a couple of movies for tonight? Give us an excuse to go into town." Sam shrugged. "Come on. You're not going to be here that much longer."

"Okay, but not a dorky family film. Let's see if we can rent Terminator or something like that."

The two boys climbed out of the tree house and went inside to find Johnny's mother. She agreed to drive them, but only after she checked with the officer who was watching the house. After last night, she was glad for the police presence. Johnny's little sister, Katie, complained about the ride into town, but the boys kept teasing her until she finally settled into a silent pout. Mrs. Mendoza dropped the boys off at the video store, and then she went down the block for milk leaving the officer behind with them.

"Man, she's treating me like a baby," Sam complained.

"She's always been overprotective," Johnny shrugged. They walked into the store and headed toward the new releases.

"How can you stand it?"

"I know she does it because she cares about me. Doesn't want me to hang out with a bad influence...like you."

"Hey!" Sam exclaimed, elbowing Johnny.

Johnny laughed. "I guess it's just the way my family is because we go to church."

"Oh," Sam said as he looked at the videos. Johnny talked about church for a little while, but Sam tuned him out. Johnny finally stopped, and they picked out a bunch of videos. They checked them out and went outside to wait for Johnny's mother to come pick them up.

Sitting on a ledge outside of the video store in sight of the police car, Sam stared off, deep in thought. Then he turned to Johnny. "I was surprised that your dad defended me last night. It was neat the way he stood up for me."

"Why wouldn't he? You didn't do anything wrong. We all know that."

"It's just...I don't think my dad would. He never stood up for me when I got in trouble at school. In the beginning, I didn't even do anything wrong. The jocks picked on me because I was the new kid. I tried to tell him that I didn't cause the trouble, but Dad never listened. After a while, I figured if I was going to get in trouble, I might as well be in trouble for stuff I actually did."

"I'm sure he would have stood up for you to the police, like Dad did last night."

"Nah, he wouldn't have. If this was Poughkeepsie, I'd already be in jail."

"But you didn't do anything. The police don't put you in jail for nothing."

"You saw the way Captain Bennett was with me until your dad stepped in. He saw my school record, so now he thinks I did something to Mrs. Peterson. Only your family stopped it."

Johnny didn't know what to say. He felt really bad for Sam. The two sat for a few moments and then Sam continued. "You said that your parents care about you 'cause they go to church. But I don't think that's what it is. My parents went to church, the same church as you when we lived here. They never really cared about me."

"Your parents care about you. How can you say that?"

Sam looked at his friend and saw the concern in Johnny's face. "When Mom was alive, she always acted like I was just a pain she had to deal with. Dad doesn't even pay attention to me. He goes to work, goes to meetings or out with Anne. Even Anne can't wait to get away from me. I know I probably deserve some of it, but Dad doesn't even like to watch TV with me like your dad does. When he is home, he avoids me."

"I fight with my parents too. All kids do."

"It's different though. I see the way your parents joke around with you, hug you." Sam shook his head and pulled his knees up. He rested his chin on his knees. "The last time my father had his arm around me or hugged me was before we left Granelle."

Johnny put his hand on his friend's shoulder. "Parents aren't perfect. They all make mistakes. Your father went through a rough time too. When you were missing, he was so upset. No one could even console him. I heard my parents talking about it."

"Too bad I was found, huh? Guess he only cared when I was lost." Sam jumped off the ledge."Here comes your mom." Johnny picked up the videos and followed Sam to the car. They were quiet on the ride back to the house. As soon as they got out of the car, Sam went to the backyard for a cigarette while Johnny brought the videos in and helped his mother with the few groceries she bought.

"What's wrong?" Mrs. Mendoza asked Johnny when they were alone.

"Sam and I were talking about parents. He thinks his father doesn't care about him."

"Well, did you tell him that wasn't true?"

"I tried to, but he told me some things that make me think maybe he has a point. Sam thinks his father would have let the police arrest him last night instead of standing up to defend him like Dad did."

"Do you want me or your father to talk to Sam?"

"No. I want him to feel like he can talk to me. This is the first time he really opened up. If he thinks I'm running to you, he won't talk. I think he really needs a friend right now that will listen to him. I just feel so bad for him. I can't imagine what it would feel like if I thought you and Dad didn't care about me." Johnny sighed. "Better get Sam and start watching these movies. I think we got too many, but at least it will keep his mind off stuff for now."

Johnny found Sam outside. Sam offered him a cigarette and Johnny shook his head. "We'd better get watching some of those movies. We got too many."

Sam smiled, "Probably did. Maybe your folks will let us stay up later tonight to watch them."

"Just as long as we don't keep them awake, it shouldn't be a problem," Johnny said, sitting on the railing that was around the deck. Sam looked past Johnny and thought he saw something. He watched and saw the dark shadow move deeper into the woods.

"Maybe we should get inside," Sam said feeling scared.

"Sure, but don't be scared yet, the movie hasn't even started," Johnny laughed. Sam followed Johnny into the house. As he glanced back to the woods, he saw the creature sitting near a tree, watching him.

CHAPTER 20

Freshly showered and wearing clean clothes, Meg stood by her washing machine trying to pull the burrs from the legs of her jeans. She had already thrown out her shirt that was torn by thorns on berry bushes. She would never tell Jake she had gone into the woods, not just because he didn't want her to, but because it had been a big waste of time and Meg was frustrated. She had hoped to at least have gotten a glimpse of the creature. Jake was probably right that Trevor wasn't staying in Granelle, but in one of the other small towns outside of Saratoga. It would be like looking for a needle in a haystack, she thought, pulling at the burrs.

Meg's house was on the outskirts of Saratoga, close to the Saratoga Performing Arts Center. On summer weekends, Meg could hear the sounds of the performances from her backyard. She had hosted several cookouts with friends, who sat in her backyard listening to the popular performers. Tonight's big name performer was already causing traffic to back up for miles on Route 50 near Meg's house.

The doorbell rang and Meg wondered if Jake could possibly be back yet. Stuffing the jeans in a hamper, Meg went to the door. She paused to look through the glass storm door. Surprised, she ran and opened the door, throwing her arms around her younger brother.

"Michael!" Meg shrieked. "What are you doing here?"

Michael hugged her back, laughing. "Well, if you would ever answer your phone, you'd know I was in town. Mom said she's been trying to call you all week."

"Come on in," she said, taking her brother's arm and leading him into the house. "Can you stay for a while?"

"Not too long. Mom's expecting me back for dinner." Michael followed Meg into the kitchen. Meg pulled out a couple of sodas out of the fridge and handed one to Michael.

"You look great," Meg said, settling in a kitchen chair. Michael had the same deep green eyes and blond hair as Meg, but with his deep California tan, olive green polo shirt, and khaki pants, Michael looked like a tourist in the town he grew up in.

"Can't beat California living," he said. "What's been going on? Got a lot of work?"

"Is this you asking or Mom?" she said opening her bottle of soda and looking sideways at her brother.

"I guess both. I was hoping that we could hang out while I'm home. Go to the track, hang out at the lake. But you haven't been answering your phone or returning messages, so I figured the only way to find out what is going on is to come over here in person."

Meg looked away and shrugged a little. "Just been tied up on a case. Nothing new."

"Nothing? Come on Meg, it's me. I come back for a visit and find out from the news that Trevor Grant has broken out of jail and is at large. Mom hasn't heard from you. I can understand your not wanting to tell Mom, but me?"

"I guess, I didn't think about telling you."

"Figured if something happened to you, we'd hear about it from the police?"

"Nothing's going to happen to me, Michael." She was getting riled. "Look, Bennett never even told me about it until days after he escaped. The department doesn't even think he's in the area."

"The whole family is concerned."

"The whole family? Who, you and Mom?

"And Dad, and Uncle George and Aunt Marcy, Stacey...."

"Okay, point taken. But I hardly think Dad cares."

"How would you even know? When was the last time you talked to him? He tells me all the time he's left you messages.." Meg didn't answer and just sat staring at the cap from the soda bottle. Michael went on. "...and your ignoring our calls is disconcerting, Meg. You were kidnapped the last time."

"You don't think I know that?" she snapped. "Don't sit here and tell me that everyone is all concerned about me. If everyone is so concerned, how come you're the only one here? How come in the past week no one has even thought to come by? If I remember correctly, the only one who even thought to check on me when I was kidnapped was Jake."

"Well, I don't see Jake here right now, do I?"

"I just saw Jake this morning, Mr. Know It All."

"Meg, I didn't come by to have a fight with you. I'm only visiting for a week. Stacey didn't even get to come with me this time. But this is the reason why

I'm the one that came. You get so defensive about everything, and lash out at everyone."

"Then why even bother coming over if I'm so awful?" Meg got up and slammed her chair into the table. Michael got up too, and met her glare.

"Because I happen to love my big sister."

Meg stood with her arms crossed. "Well, you shouldn't have bothered. I can take care of myself."

"Can you? It sounds like the first sign of trouble sends you running to Jake. He's married to someone else now."

"Why do you feel the need to state the obvious to me?"

"Oh, my God, Meg. What is wrong with you? You constantly push the family away from you. We weren't the ones who hurt you...."

"Don't psychoanalyze me. I'm not one of your patients."

"Well, maybe you should be. I think you really need counseling."

Meg stared at Michael and then shook her head. "Just go back to Mom's. I don't need this now."

"I want to help you."

"How? How do you think you can possibly help me? Can you find out where Grant is hiding? Do you know where I can find Sam Craig? Do you know where that creature is stalking again? Do you have any clue what started this whole nightmare again? Because if you can't answer those questions, there is nothing you can do to help me."

"Do you even hear yourself? You aren't a cop anymore. What are you doing?"

"I'll tell you what I'm doing. I'm trying to protect myself by finding Grant before he finds me."

"Meg," Michael said in a quiet, patient voice. "I know that you are an investigator. But you are too close to this."

"Look, I have to do this. I need to have control over this situation."

"Is that why? Because you want to control the investigation?" When Meg didn't answer Michael went on in a softer voice. "We come from a family of cops, remember? You shouldn't be near this investigation."

"I'm not near the investigation," Meg said, sitting back down and playing with her soda. "Jake and I are looking on our own."

"This isn't good, Meg. Jake shouldn't be anywhere near this either since it's his wife that is missing. Does Bennett know what you two are up to?"

"No, and you better not say anything to him."

"Why not? I'm afraid for you. If you're looking for Grant, you're going to put yourself right in harm's way."

"We can handle this together. We were good partners before, and we will be that again."

Michael studied her for a moment, making her feel uncomfortable. She finally looked away. "Please, Meg, if you won't go to Bennett, at least talk to Dad about this."

"No, I'm going to be fine."

"It isn't going to stop me from worrying about you," Michael said firmly. "Look, I won't go to the police because I know how you feel about Bennett, but I'm going to tell Dad what you're doing and let him figure out what to do."

"Dad will just go to Bennett. Dad never wanted me to even be a cop...."

"I know all of that. Dad already figured out that you were doing something on your own."

"How? There's no way he could know."

"He told me that if he was in your shoes, he would be doing just what you are. He just didn't figure that Jake would be involved."

Meg stared at Michael and then shook her head. "No way. Dad is too by the book. He would never...."

"Yeah, he would. He even told me about a few times when he broke the rules just to prove to me he has."

"Let's say I believe you. So what?"

"Dad wants to talk to you. He figured you wouldn't go to him on your own, so he asked me to talk to you."

"I can't go to Dad. We don't get along."

"Dad and you don't get along because you are two of a kind. He's proud of you and wants to help you."

They stood staring at each other, Michael waiting for Meg to give in. Finally, she sighed and looked away. "Okay, I'll call him tomorrow."

"I might be younger than you, but I wasn't born yesterday. You never call people when you say you will. We're actually having dinner at Dad's tonight. They have a place for you."

"No. I will not have dinner with that woman...."

"You mean our stepmother? She's not the villain Mom portrays her to be. If you just get to know her, she's really a nice person. Now, get your shoes on or we are going to be late for dinner."

"I'll just call him. Right now, so you can see me do it." Meg got up and reached for her phone.

"Come on, Meg. This really isn't a conversation to have on the phone. You should talk to Dad face to face."

"I don't want to do this."

"I know you don't, but if you don't go to him, he's planning on coming here. I think it would be easier on you if you go with me, so I can be there for you."

"You think I need my little brother to protect me from my father?"

"Not protect. But sometimes you and Dad need a referee."

"Michael, I don't want to talk to Dad."

"I'll give you a choice. You can talk to Dad or I'll talk to Captain Bennett. Dad won't arrest you; Bennett will."

"Seriously? You would go to Bennett?"

"That's how worried I am about you. And I'll tell him Jake is involved too."

"This is blackmail."

"Come on, Meg. Dad's not your enemy...he's just Dad."

A couple of hours later, Meg was sitting in her father's den. Her stepmother, Rachel, and Michael were cleaning up the dinner dishes. Her father, Brian, had been watching his daughter all through dinner. It had been a couple of years since he had seen Meg; the last time was just after his marriage to Rachel. Brian had been a police officer first in Saratoga, and then Albany when his marriage to his kids' mother ended badly. Brian had pulled Michael aside to find out how involved Meg was, and he wasn't surprised to hear she was investigating on her own.

"So, how are things in Saratoga these days?" Brian began tentatively.

"Dad, I know you didn't ask me over to talk about Saratoga."

"You're right, I didn't. What can I do to help?" he asked.

Meg looked at her father. "Aren't you going to yell at me first? Tell me that I'm making a mistake?"

"Meggie, if it was up to me, I'd be putting you on the next plane to California and hiding you at Michael's. But I doubt you'll go. Am I right?"

"You're right. I'm not leaving until I see Grant dead or back behind bars."

"Is anything I say going to stop you from going after Grant?"

"No." she said firmly, crossing her arms.

"I knew you wouldn't. You're too much like me," Brian said, smiling at Meg.

"I'm nothing like you," she said defiantly. In fact, she was. She got her hard-headedness from her father, but her looks from her mother.

"Right." Brian chuckled. "Now tell me what you plan to do and what you know."

"I don't believe this," Meg said. "Do you really think I'm going to tip my hand so you can run to Bennett?"

"Meggie, I might be a cop, but not in Granelle. I don't answer to Reggie Bennett." Meg stared defiantly at her father. The years apart didn't leave her room for trusting her father now. When she didn't respond, Brian went on. "Look, Meggie, I know that I haven't always been the best father in the world. But I'm a cop. I can help you in ways that no one else can because I have access to police files."

"Don't call me, Meggie. And I already know what kind of father you are."

"Well, what do you say? Want the old man to help you with your investigation?"

"I already have a partner helping me," she said, sticking her chin out. "I don't need any others in the mix."

"I know Jake is helping you. But he's not on the force either. There is information only I can get for you. Besides, Jake shouldn't be involved."

Meg just looked away from her father's gaze. She knew all the reasons why Jake shouldn't be involved. And she knew she shouldn't be involved either. "Jake won't be talked out of this either. This is way too personal to both of us."

"I know. That's the thing that scares me the most. So you need me. I can be levelheaded about this. I get why you want to find Grant and that you are a good investigator. But you need to look at this objectively and remember that Sarah's life is in your hands if you get yourself involved."

"This isn't about Sarah. This is about finding Grant."

"You're wrong, Meg," Brian said quietly. "Sarah matters more than anyone else right now. How can you, of all people, forget what it felt like to be held prisoner by that man? How can you forget those things, knowing right now, that Sarah is experiencing those very things?"

"I get it, Dad. Okay. But I don't want you involved. You'll lose your job if the force finds out."

"I care more about you. Now, as it happens, I already know a lot about the case because I looked at the files. But what else is going on that you or Jake haven't told the police?"

"I can't tell you those things," Meg said, looking down at her hands. "Not unless I talk to Jake first."

"Ask Jake to come over here and talk to me too."

"No, I'll call him first and see if it's okay. Besides he's probably not even back yet."

"Back from where?" Brian asked.

"None of your business," Meg said, smirking at him. "If he wants you to know, he'll need to tell you."

Meg went out on the back door with her cell phone. She talked to Jake briefly and they agreed to meet at her office in the morning. Meg hung up and stood on the back deck. She leaned on the railing and enjoyed just relaxing. For a few fleeting seconds, she considered the freedom of going to California with Michael. Getting away, maybe not to Michael's, but maybe here, if Dad was going to help and Rachel wasn't as bad as Mom said. Maybe a few nights here. A few nights' sleep, knowing she was safe.

CHAPTER 21

The creature watched Sam through the sliding glass doors that led to the family room. Sam could see the glowing eyes watching and couldn't concentrate on the movie. Instead, he was drawn over and over again to the window. He remembered what Trevor had said all those years ago, that if Sam ever betrayed his friendship to him, the creature would know, and it would go after Sam. Yet, Sam remembered that the creature had attacked Trevor in the end. Sam was just a kid back then and was really scared.

Sam thought he remembered challenging Trevor saying that he, not Trevor, was the keeper of the creatures. Sam looked at the scar on his finger and rubbed it. He clearly remembered getting bitten. He got up and went back to the window.

"Okay, what gives?" Johnny paused the movie.

"Huh?" Sam said, turning to Johnny.

"Is the movie that lame that you're not interested? You picked this one out."

"Oh, it's nothing. I guess I just keep thinking about Trevor being out there someplace." Sam came back to the couch.

"Do you want something to eat?"

"Sure," Sam said, distracted. When Johnny got up to go into the kitchen, Sam went to window again. He looked over his shoulder to be sure that Johnny wasn't there, and then slipped out the sliding glass doors. He looked up to the deck where the door from the kitchen was and didn't see Johnny there either. He pulled a cigarette out and lit it, watching the creature just inside the woods. The creature lay down and put his head on its paws.

Sam looked back into the room and then walked toward the tree house. Keeping his eyes on the creature, he walked quickly just in case it came at him. He stuck his cigarette in his mouth and climbed up the ladder to the tree house. Feeling safer, he began to speak.

"Okay, I hope you can understand me. Johnny is my friend and so is his family. So that means you can't do anything to them. I don't know why you showed up now. Are you here to protect me from Trevor? Or to get me for Trevor?"

The creature cocked its head to one side as if understanding Sam. "I guess this is kind of stupid talking to you. But I think I remember something about that time. I think you saved me from Trevor."

The creature was suddenly alert and quietly slipped back a few paces. He lay down behind a log and some dead leaves. If Sam didn't know he was there, he would never have seen him. Johnny came out to the tree house.

"You should have said you wanted to smoke. My mom just about freaked when you weren't in the family room," Johnny said while climbing up.

"I'm not used to being treated like this. Nobody usually cares what I do. Want one?" Sam offered Johnny a cigarette.

"Naw, I don't think I'm going to keep smoking. If I don't stop, I'll be hooked like you."

"Yeah, probably," Sam said, flicking his cigarette onto the ground below.

"Mom said to tell you to stop flicking your butts into the yard. That's what this is for." Johnny grabbed an old coffee can.

"You brought that out days ago. Why didn't you tell me then?"

"I didn't want you to think I was a wuss."

"Too late for that," Sam said, as Johnny punched him.

"Seriously, man. Mom says we have to pick up all the butts too."

Sam just shook his head. "Wuss."

"So, you ready to go back in yet?" Johnny said, starting to get up.

"Naw, you can go if you want though."

"It's okay. The movie's lame anyway." He sat back down. He let his long legs hang over the side of the tree house.

"I don't think I can take all this overprotection. Do you think we could take a walk into the woods?"

"You serious?"

"Sure, why not? We did it a few days ago. Trevor was loose then and nothing happened."

"No way. I'll be surprised if they let us do anything else alone the rest of your visit."

"This is dumb. We're both almost eighteen."

"Sorry, but my folks feel responsible for you."

"Don't they realize that if Trevor wants to get me, they won't be able to stop him?"

"I don't think I want to go into the woods right now anyway."

"Come on. I feel like I'm being punished. Can't we just ask your father and see if we can take a walk? Even if it's just on the road? Or ride to town and get pizza?"

"I guess we can ask," Johnny said hesitantly, "but he probably won't let us do it tonight. It's getting kind of late."

"Tomorrow is fine. I just can't stand being watched all the time. Let's go ask him."

Sam got up and Johnny reluctantly followed. He didn't see a major problem with them going out in the daytime, but his parents would probably find something to object to. As Sam waited for Johnny to climb down, he looked back to the woods. The creature was still there watching Sam.

The boys went into the house and found Mr. Mendoza watching television in his bedroom. He muted the TV when they came in. Johnny sat on the bed and Sam sat in the only chair in the room. Johnny hesitated, so Sam took over.

"I told Johnny how surprised I was that you stood up for me the other night with Captain Bennett. My dad wouldn't have done that."

"It was easy to stand up for you knowing you had no part in Mrs. Peterson's disappearance. I'm sure your father would have done that, Sam," Mr. Mendoza responded.

"Johnny said the same thing. But I know he wouldn't have. Dad never was a strong person. He didn't want me to come to Granelle because he thought coming here would bring back a lot of bad memories for me. But he let Anne and me badger him into letting me come. He was right in some ways, like seeing my old house, having my old friends treat me like dirt, especially Melinda. I've had bad dreams being here about those days when I was locked in the basement at the Hanson house. I wake up in the middle of the night afraid until I realize where I am. I wanted to leave."

"Has it been that bad here?" Johnny seemed a little hurt.

"In some ways, yeah. I even called my Aunt Sheryl and my sister, Karen. They said that I couldn't go to their houses. Made me feel pretty worthless, like no one wants me."

Johnny started to say something, but Mr. Mendoza put his hand up to stop him. "Go on, Sam."

Sam hesitated, looking at Johnny. "The other day, I was going to lie to you and tell you that Dad came back early. I was going to just go home. But you've been so nice to me that I found I couldn't lie to you. Then Captain Bennett showed up. You stood up for me. Johnny, when you came into the kitchen and sat down next to me, it made me realize what a good friend you are." Sam stopped, as he was getting a little choked up.

"Sam," Mr. Mendoza began, "I didn't know you were going through all of this."

"I thought it was going to be so different coming back here. I thought it would be like before all the bad stuff happened."

"I'm glad that you finally came and talked to me. Is there something more you need to say?"

Sam thought about the dark creature watching him from the woods. "It's just...I'm not really used to being so close to home all the time. I don't really understand when we're almost eighteen. I know that Trevor's out there somewhere, but I feel claustrophobic. Can we just drive in to town and get some pizza tomorrow? I just need to get out."

Mr. Mendoza looked over at Johnny. "How do you feel about this?"

"A little like Sam does. I'm used to driving myself around and hanging out with my friends. I'm scared though, about us running into Trevor," Johnny said.

"But what are the chances of running into Trevor in the middle of Granelle in broad daylight? He's not a stupid person," Sam countered.

"I'm glad you both felt like you could ask me, but I have to say no. Besides, the police won't let you either," Mr. Mendoza said.

Sam sighed and shook his head, "I hate this. But I have another question. Can I be allowed to smoke in the backyard alone again? Johnny doesn't smoke, and I'll pick up all the butts."

"You'll pick up the butts either way. I know Johnny's smoked since you've been here."

Johnny looked ashamed. "Dad...I'm not going to anymore. I don't even like it."

"So why did Sam just say that you don't smoke?"

"I just told him today, I wasn't going to smoke anymore. I don't want to get hooked."

"Good decision," Mr. Mendoza said. "What about you, Sam?"

"Me?" Sam said with surprise. "I've been smoking for a couple of years already. I'm sorry I had Johnny try it."

"Fair enough." He got up. "My concern about you being outside alone is that you mentioned some animal being out there."

Sam stood too. "I don't know what I really saw. But it was the middle of the night, too. We had just watched some scary movies."

"Well, I need to give this some thought. Probably better to not smoke in the middle of the night either way. I'll let you know my decision later. For now, start picking up those butts while there's still some daylight left."

"Thanks for listening," Sam said.

The boys went outside to clean up the cigarette butts. Sam checked the woods and didn't see the creature anymore. But he figured he was out there in the woods somewhere. Soon, he would find out just which side it was on, his or Trevor's.

CHAPTER 22

Jake had a restless night. He didn't know what to think of the risk that Brian Riley was willing to take by wanting to help them find Grant. Although it was still early, Jake finally gave up on trying to sleep anymore. He took a long, hot shower and fixed a cup of coffee. Sitting in the kitchen, he read his Bible and prayed while drinking the coffee. The early morning sun began to shine into the kitchen and Buddy padded in, whining to go out.

Jake took the dog outside and sat in his chair watching him. The early morning was warm and the dew was already evaporating. Jake walked back to the wood line to see if there were any new prints in the soft dirt. There was nothing new, but Jake poked around in the woods for a while with Buddy right beside him. Buddy started following a scent deeper into the woods, and Jake called him back. It was getting late, and Jake wanted to get to Saratoga to meet Meg.

After putting Buddy back in the house and leaving food and water for his pets, Jake left to meet Meg. He got to Saratoga and found a parking spot right in front of Meg's office. He walked up the stairs to her office, tried the door, and found it locked. He was about to leave when he heard a noise inside. Jake knocked again and called out.

"Who is it?" a voice called.

"It's Jake," he replied. He heard banging around inside and the door was unlocked. Meg stood before him looking rumpled, and he noticed the blanket on the love seat in the reception area. "Did you spend the night here?"

"Yeah, it was kind of late when I left Dad's and he had me spooked. I figured in the summer, Saratoga is always busy and I would be safe here. Come on in. I'll call down to the restaurant and see if they can send up some coffee and bagels."

Jake went into the office and folded up the blanket while Meg went into her office and made the call. He set the folded blanket on the love seat.

"Hey, Jake, come on in here," Meg called out. "I thought we should start by going over everything we know and figure out where the holes are. That way we will be able...."

Jake started walking into her office when the outer door opened. He looked surprised as Brian walked in. "Meg, what's going on?" Jake asked.

"What do you mean?" Meg asked, coming toward Jake. She saw her father and stopped.

"Meggie didn't know I was coming this morning," Brian said, closing the office door.

"Dad, what are you doing here?" Meg pushed past Jake.

"I figured if I waited for an invitation, it wouldn't come. But I overheard you talking to Jake last night and decided to come here and talk to both of you at the same time."

"Well, leave," Meg said, pointing at the door.

"Wait, maybe he should stay." Jake went back and sat on the love seat. "I keep thinking about you going off into the woods yesterday."

"Jake, I told you it was a waste of time. It's ridiculous to think this is why my father should be involved."

"I told you last night that I think we are both reacting too quickly to things. You know, not thinking through the consequences of acting alone."

Meg cut him off. "That was the problem. We were acting alone. Now we have each other and...."

"Each other?" Brian asked. He sat down in the chair by the desk.

"Dad, stay out of this. This is our decision to make, not yours." Meg was trying to dismiss him.

But Brian wouldn't stop. "Jake, I'm sorry to hear about your wife. I know that if this was Rachel, I would want to comb the town myself to find her."

Jake nodded. "That's how I feel. But I don't think we are going to find Sarah in Granelle. I think it's too risky for Grant to have her there."

"Are you sure that Grant has her? There aren't any other suspects?" Brian continued.

Meg was exasperated and tried to interrupt. But Jake just answered Brian's questions. "I know for sure that it's Grant. He called me at the church the other night."

"What does he want?"

"Why are you answering his questions?" Meg interrupted. "We haven't said we would work with Dad. We can handle this ourselves, and honestly, I don't want to get him in any trouble." Someone knocked on the door. Brian jumped up quickly and drew his gun, standing next to the door. "Will you relax," Meg said, "I ordered coffee and bagels."

"You need to be careful," Brian whispered. She sighed and went to the door. The kid told her how much the order was and Meg pulled out money and handed it to him. He went to give her change and she waved him off. She closed the door and showed her father.

"Satisfied, Dad? What were you going to do? Shoot the delivery boy?" Meg walked to Allison's desk and set down the bag of bagels and the coffees.

"So, do you need any more time to think about this?" Brian asked Jake.

"This isn't an easy answer to give you. On one hand, I think we could use the help," Jake began.

"Jake, don't tell him that," Meg said, tearing a bagel in half.

"Well, it's the truth. I'd feel better knowing your father was involved. Between you going off half cocked into the woods yesterday, knowing full well that it was extremely dangerous to do, and me driving around Saratoga looking for Doug after Reggie gives me a little information, it might be wise. He's at least still an officer."

"That's a good point," Brian said, taking a bagel himself. Meg swatted his hand.

"But," Jake said with caution, "this is putting you at risk. Somehow, Trevor's been watching me. That could put you in harm's way. And how will the department look at this if your involvement comes out?"

"My daughter, my problem." Brian chomped on the bagel.

"Not your problem," Meg said. "I'm your grown daughter, who is voting against your help."

"Look, you two might be ex-cops, but I'm still the real McCoy here. I've got access, and I've got friends who would do anything for me," Brian countered.

"Great, let's get more police involved that shouldn't be, so I can feel more guilty," Jake murmured.

"What's to feel guilty about, Jake? I'm offering to help. You aren't forcing me. But if I'm in, I'm in all the way. You need to tell me everything and what you need."

"What we need, Dad, is some privacy. Go home," Meg took a tentative sip of her coffee and sat down on Allison's desk.

"Wait, Meg," Jake said. "I get a say in this, too."

Brian finished the bagel, went over to the love seat and sat down next to Jake. "Listen," he began. "Meg told me that she told you this is about finding Grant. I don't know how you responded. But this isn't about Grant, this is about Sarah. I remember the long recovery that two of those women faced after they were found the last time. I know the longer she is gone, the more her condition is going to deteriorate. We need to move fast to save her."

"That's not fair," Meg said, jumping off the desk. "You're going to have Jake making this decision based on his emotions."

"That's all it is about anyway," Jake said despondently. "Mr. Riley, I'd be glad to have your help. We just found out the day before she disappeared that Sarah is pregnant. I can't imagine the effects this will have on the baby if she is being drugged."

"Then the sooner we get to work, the sooner she'll be home," Brian said.

Meg made a call to Allison, giving her the day off with pay. Then they moved into the small conference room next to her office. Brian took a pen from Allison's desk and grabbed some paper from her printer. "Let's start at the beginning. Tell me everything you both know."

Less than an hour later, Meg and Brian were fighting and Jake finally had to stop them. "Maybe you two should work on separate aspects of the case," Jake said, sitting in a chair between them.

"Okay," Meg said, frustrated by the whole process. "I'll keep looking for Sam. Call the papers in Poughkeepsie and see if any wedding announcements are coming out for Stanley and his new wife. See if I can find Karen Craig. She would have to know where Sam is staying."

"What is your excuse going to be for wanting to know where Sam is?" Brian asked.

"The truth. Grant's loose and we want to be sure he's all right," Meg said. "What about you, Jake, what do you want to work on?"

"I want to find out more about the letters. Maybe the attorney that sent the letter to Grant knows something about him that we can use, like places he used to stay and stuff about the past. I can use that for leverage when Grant calls me back."

"I'll look at the police records and see if there is anything new," Brian said. "We've gotten so that more and more case notes are computerized."

"Will they know you've accessed the records?" Jake was concerned. "I don't want to raise any red flags."

"No, I've got a buddy in records," he replied. "I'll tell him I am worried about my daughter and just want to see if anyone knows if Grant is in town."

Meg grunted. "Yeah, like that's believable!"

"Sure it is," Brian said. "I'm always asking about you. Everyone on the force knows how much I care about you."

"Dad, this is the first time in years we've talked. No one is going to believe you," Meg said. Jake was going to say something, but waited.

"It doesn't matter that we haven't talked. You're still my daughter. I still care about you, keep track of you, know what's going on in your life. I'm your father. My friends always knew that I kept tabs on you. Not only through Michael, but also your mother."

Meg stared at her father for a few long moments, then got up and left the room. They heard her office door slam. Jake started to say something, but Brian shook his head, got up, and left Jake alone in the conference room. Jake figured they all could use a break right now anyway.

CHAPTER 23

Sam peeked around the side of the house to make sure there was no one watching. With Officer Greg having a cup of coffee with Mrs. Mendoza, Sam thought this was the perfect time to sneak away. He turned and gestured to Johnny to follow him toward his car. Sam went to the driver's side and quietly opened the door. He stepped on the clutch, put the car into neutral, and with Johnny's help, they pushed the car to into the road. Once they were out of sight of the house, Sam slipped behind the wheel. Johnny jumped in the passenger side as Sam started the car.

"YAY!" Sam yelled as he drove away. Sam was relieved and excited to be away from watching eyes. Even a few hours out of the house would be great for Sam.

"Glad you're so happy," Johnny said with a huge smile. "But I'm going to get grounded for this."

"Yeah, but doesn't it feel great?" Sam said laughing. "FREEDOM!"

Johnny laughed. "It does feel great! I've never done anything like this before."

"I do this kind of stuff all the time."

"I figured that, it's just...." Johnny trailed off.

"Go ahead, I know what I am. I'm one of those bad kids. But at least I'm not a geek like you," Sam said, still laughing.

"Don't, Sam. You aren't what you think you are. Yeah, we've both changed into different people. But the past few days, I can see you're still Sam. My friend. Regardless of what's happened, how different we are, you're still one of my best friends."

"Yeah, I know what you mean," Sam said. "It's cool that we're still friends."

"Hey, I was wondering something. What do you think is going to happen when you get home?"

"What'd you mean?" Sam asked as he drove toward town.

"What if they don't find Trevor before you leave? Do you think your Dad is going to let you go out alone?"

"Why not?"

"You don't think he'd be worried about Trevor finding you again?" Johnny looked at Sam. He saw the hardened look in Sam's eyes and quickly went on. "I was thinking maybe you should just stay with us."

"What? Stay here in Granelle?"

"Sure. It would be fun."

"Naw, I don't think I can take this much longer. I'm used to a lot more freedom than you get." Sam pulled into a parking place in the middle of town.

"Sam, I don't want anything to happen to you. You can stay and finish your senior year here in Granelle."

"I hate to burst your bubble, but I don't think I'm going back to school. My grades were bad and I don't have enough credits to graduate anyway."

"So what? You can stay and get your GED. You can do it online or at the community college."

"How do you know so much about getting a GED already?"

"I've been checking into it and talking to my Dad."

Sam just looked at Johnny. "I'd have to think about this. I doubt my father will care either way."

"Okay." Johnny and Sam got out of the car. "So Sam, what else can we do to get in trouble? Might as well make this trip worth it."

Sam laughed. "Slow down, bud. Let's just get some pizza. Then I thought I'd like to go by my old house."

They walked down the sidewalk toward the pizza place. It was packed, and they had to wait, so they played a few video games. Finally, they were able to get a booth. Once they got their pizza, Johnny went back to the idea of Sam staying. "If you did go back, what would you do?"

"Probably just get a job," Sam said, taking a bite of his pizza.

"What kind?"

"I don't know. I'd have to see what's around. I'm moving out as soon as I'm eighteen anyway, so I've got to be able to pay for rent."

"You've already thought about this?"

"Dad's got a new wife. He's not going to want me hangin' around." Sam was losing interest in his pizza. "Why do you have to talk about this? I wanted to have some fun today."

"Sorry. I just want to really look at all your options. I want you to stay."

"You think you want me to stay. You don't think I'm going to get on your nerves after a while? You don't think I won't have fights with your parents? I'm used to being alone. I'm used to having my own space."

"Being alone isn't all that great a choice either."

"I told you I'd think about it, maybe talk to your Dad. But don't push it, Johnny. This is what I'm used to whether you think it's such a great life or not. It's just what is. Let's get out of here."

"Hey, at least let me eat!" Johnny said, cramming pizza into his mouth. "Besides, we just have to go back to the house anyway."

"Naw, I'm not ready yet. I still want to go past my old house."

"I don't want to get in trouble," Johnny said, quickly finishing his lunch.

"We're already in trouble. I thought you wanted to have fun. We could snoop around my old house and see what those people did to change it. Come on, don't be a drag." Sam stood up and headed for the door.

"Okay, okay," Johnny got up and followed Sam out. "Don't get your shorts into a bunch."

"Old and tired, man. You aren't cut out to be a bad kid," Sam punched Johnny in the shoulder. He threw out the rest of his pizza and took his soda with him.

Sam and Johnny walked back to the car, joking around. Johnny's cell phone rang, and both boys moaned. "Hello," Johnny said answering. "Yeah, Dad, we're fine....we just went for some pizza...Nothing...I know...but..." There was a long pause while Johnny listened. Finally he said, "We're headed home right now."

"Guess he's mad?" Sam asked, opening the car door.

"He was yelling at me. Next time, just believe me." Johnny got in the passenger side.

"Hey, if I did that, we wouldn't be here right now," Sam said. "You were having fun, remember?"

"Tell that to my ear," Johnny said, laughing. Sam laughed with him and started the car. "But seriously, we're in big trouble."

"And you want me to live with your family? Right!"

"Sam, Dad said that Trevor was seen in a store in Saratoga. The U.S. Marshals are coming to take us to a safe house."

"I'm not going back." There was finality in his voice.

"I don't think this is open to discussion. He said we had to get home and pack."

"Bad enough that we've had 'Officer Greg' lurking around the house, I'm not going to any safe house with real cops."

"You don't have any choice."

"Yeah, I do. We don't have to go back. We can just take off."

"We? I can't just run away. My father will flip out."

The boys didn't talk for a few minutes as Sam drove out of town. Finally Sam said, "I understand your wanting to stay. Your dad's been nice about everything. But I can't stay. The cops all look at me like I did something to Mrs. Peterson."

"Dad already fixed all that. Don't leave."

"It's more than just that. If I stay, I put your whole family in danger. The only way to protect you is to leave. I'll be okay. I'm used to being alone."

"Sam..." Johnny started, but Sam pulled over to the side of the road.

"You've been the best friend I could ever ask for. I know how dangerous Trevor can be and I can't put you in that kind of danger." Sam shuddered. "If I'm with you, he will hurt you to get to me."

"What makes you think he's even after you?"

"Because of that creature."

"Dad said it's just a big wolf. The rest is just a myth." Johnny looked around at the surrounding woods.

"You've got to believe me. Look," Sam said, showing Johnny the scar on his hand. "When I was held in that basement, that creature bit me. How can a myth bite me?"

"A wolf can bite you. I didn't say the wolf part wasn't real."

"Maybe I'm wrong. I was a kid. But Trevor told me stuff about that animal. It was smart and it was like it could understand me when I talked to it."

"Okay, if you're right about it, the police will protect you from Trevor and that creature."

"That's the thing, I don't think I need to be protected from the creature. I think somehow, I'm meant to be with it. I think that it was watching me in Poughkeepsie too. I remember seeing the eyes at night. I almost feel safe knowing it's watching me."

"Okay." Johnny finally relented. "How are you going to get away? Obviously, they are going to be waiting for us to get back."

"If you don't mind walking back, I can just leave from here. That way they can't follow me."

"Walk back? You want me to believe you about some creature being in Granelle and then want me to walk?" Johnny was incredulous.

"This is going to sound weird, but if it knows you're my friend, it won't hurt you."

"I don't get it, Sam."

"Do you remember when I was kidnapped, Trevor had taken those women and two escaped from the Hanson house?"

"Of course I remember."

"I told them when they were leaving that if the creature knew they were friends of mine, he wouldn't hurt them. I gave them an old blanket that I had been using in the basement. When they were found by the police, the one woman told me that I saved their lives. The creature followed them all the way down that road and kept Trevor from finding them."

"So what?"

"Don't you see? My scent was on that blanket, and it knew that they were my friends. That creature knows you're my friend. It's been watching us together. And if I give you my shirt, he will know my scent."

"That's supposed to make me feel safe? Your stinky shirt?"

Sam stared out into the woods. Finally he said, "I can't go back, Johnny. I need to be with that creature. He is the only thing that can protect me from Trevor. I know it. The police are just going to make me a sitting target."

"I think you're making a big mistake."

"Maybe I am. But I'm trying to protect your family from Trevor. You don't have to be afraid of the creature."

"All right, but I don't like you just leaving like this. And don't give me your shirt." Johnny made a face. "It really does stink."

"Okay, but I need to give you something," Sam said with a crooked smile. He looked in the backseat and pulled out an old duffel bag. "Sure you don't want my shirt? These are my gym clothes that have been here since school got out in June." Sam laughed as he opened the bag and pulled out some dirty clothes.

"Man! You suck. Just give me the empty bag." Johnny took the bag as Sam dropped the dirty clothes in the backseat. "I don't know what I'm going to say to my parents or the police."

Johnny opened his door and started getting out. Sam stopped him. "Thanks for everything. I'll call you when I know it's safe."

"You'd better." Johnny got out. He stood on the side of the road and watched as Sam turned the car around and drove away.

Johnny looked down the road both ways and opted to cut through the woods. His cell phone rang and he ignored it. He'd be home soon anyway. It was muggy and hot in the woods. Johnny kept his head down and tried to think of how to explain that Sam was gone. He climbed up a little embankment and looked down into his backyard. He heard a noise in the woods and turned to see a dark figure coming toward him.

Johnny stood with his hand on his hips trying to place the familiar person. As the figure got closer to Johnny, he realized who it was. Dropping Sam's bag, he turned to run to the house hollering, but was quickly overcome. After a brief struggle, Trevor picked up the lanky boy and carried him deep into the woods.

CHAPTER 24

Jake got off the phone feeling frustrated. He had spent hours making calls and lists and was no closer to finding anything to help them find Grant...and Sarah. Brian came rushing into the office and came into the conference room. Jake looked up expectantly.

"I got some information from....where's Meg? She should hear this." Brian left the room to find Meg.

Brian came back in with Meg, who was still looking mad. She sat in a chair glaring at her father. Crossing her arms, she slouched down in the chair.

"As I was about to tell Jake, there's a lot of stuff going on in the case locally," Brian began. "But the police are keeping everything from the press."

"Do they have any information about Sarah?" Jake said hopefully.

"No, sorry. But they did tail you and Doug. They followed him right to New Rochelle. There is surveillance on him. He is still a suspect in Sarah's case. Bennett thinks he really duped you."

"I don't agree with Reggie about Doug. I spent the past few days with him and know that he had nothing to do with Sarah."

"Okay, let's get to stuff I do know. When I looked into the computer files, there's nothing there. The whole thing looks like it's Elmira's case. But I had one of my old friends dig up some stuff. His old partner is working in Granelle. He's been poking around and overheard Bennett talking about the case. Bennett's doing most of the work himself, keeping it close. You know what I mean?"

"So how does this help us?" Meg asked.

"Because he talks a lot. You did see the boy that day in Saratoga. He's staying with a family in Granelle."

Meg stood up. "I knew it! You have the address? Let's get over there...."

"Hold on a minute," Brian said. "Just sit right back down. He's not accessible to you."

"Then what are we supposed to do?" Meg said as she sank back down in her seat.

"Problem is that Grant's here too. He was spotted in one of the shops in Saratoga."

"Saratoga? Where?" Meg jumped up again.

"Megan Katharine Riley, sit down and stop being so impatient. You don't have all the facts on anything and you're ready to run all over the place." Meg scowled and sat again. "Out of your system yet?"

"Brian, don't," Jake said quietly. "I feel just like Meg. I want to do something. Sitting here making calls that give me no information feels like such a big waste. Now knowing Sam and Grant are both here in Granelle...." Jake shook his head. "It's almost too much going on to be true."

"Well, it is true. My buddy saw the photo from the security camera. It's really Grant. Problem is that's all they have on him. They can't find where he is staying."

"At least if and when Grant calls me back," said Jake, "I can say that I know Sam is in Granelle."

"You can't tell him that," Meg said. "He'll just go get him. You can't trade Sam for Sarah."

"Then what am I supposed to do, Meg? He said he was going to kill her if I don't give him something."

"There's not too much you can do, Jake," Brian said. "The whole thing is going to be out of Bennett's hands soon. The U.S. Marshals are coming to remove the boy and the family he's staying with and take them into protective custody."

"And that's supposed to help Sarah?" Jake was getting upset. "What about her life?"

"There's part of our problem. You never reported this to the police. They don't know that there's been an offer of Sam for Sarah. They're just moving the boy because Trevor's in the area."

"What should I do? Should I go to Bennett?" Jake asked, looking at Brian.

It was Meg who quickly answered. "No. He said he'd kill her. Besides, we are the ones who should get Grant. This was our case."

"Meggie, this isn't your case," Brian said. "If the U.S. Marshals are involved, it's probably time for us to go to the police. It's a different set of rules with them."

"You're wrong, Dad. It's the same. Grant is after us."

"All the more reason to cut it loose. Let the Marshals get him. They have the same objective you do, to get Grant back in jail."

"That's not my objective. My objective is to see that man dead." Meg's voice was steel. Hate and bitterness were in her eyes. Jake stared at her and then stood up.

"I think I need to leave," he said as he gathered up the papers he had in front of him.

"Why? We know where everyone is now. We just need to...." Meg started. She put her hands on top of the papers Jake was trying to pile.

"We just need to what, Meg? I never signed on to kill anyone. I just want my wife back alive," Jake said sadly. "If you even thought for one minute that I was here to help you murder a man, you were wrong. I want to go home."

"What are you going to do? Call Bennett?" Meg was not backing down.

"Meggie, let him go," Brian said.

"It's all right, Brian," Jake said. He left the papers where they were and walked to the door. "I don't really know what I'm going to do, Meg. I'm afraid to tell Reggie because of what Grant said. I just don't know what to do."

Meg followed him. "The right thing to do is to get him before he gets us."

Jake turned, furious. "Gets us? I'd gladly give my life to save Sarah's and our unborn child. Don't you get it? This is about saving her life, nothing else."

"And I told you when all this started, it was about getting Grant," Meg shouted at Jake.

Jake stared at her and shook his head. "It's over Meg. There's nothing more we can do."

Jake walked to the door. She grabbed his arm and stopped him. "Don't leave. We have to stay here and figure this out. He's got to be close and if we get him, we'll find Sarah."

Jake shook her off, opened the door, and walked out. Meg stood staring at the door for a minute and then turned around. Her father stood in the doorway to the conference room. "I'm still here, Meg. I'm not going to stop helping you if you want to keep on looking for Grant."

"I'm not stopping." Meg crossed her arms.

"Let's get back to work then. Catch me up on what you know."

"What if Jake talks to Bennett?"

"I don't think he will...at least not tonight. Let's just see if we can figure out where Grant might be."

Meg turned away from the door and went into the conference room with her father. Brian watched his daughter as she took Jake's notes and began to read them. He could feel her anger and frustration.

"Meg," Brian said, putting his hand on her arm. "I think we should talk."

"Look, I'm sorry I got so mad before," Meg started. Brian waved her off.

"Meggie, it's more than just you being mad about today. Things haven't been right between us for years. Then last night, I handled things wrong. I thought if I could just push my way into your life, we'd be fine."

"It's not really that simple."

"I just don't understand what happened between us."

"What don't you understand? You walked out of my life."

"I didn't leave you, I left your mother."

Tears filled up in Meg's eyes. "No, Dad, you left me too."

"Honey, things were really bad between me and your mother. We were fighting all the time."

"I know, I was there, but your being there made it all right. After you left, Mom was unstable. I had to protect Michael," Meg whispered as she wiped the tears from her eyes.

"I was always there for you. You just had to call me. You and Michael could have lived with me..."

"Oh, Daddy, I couldn't. What would have happened to Mom if we had left?"

"Your mother would have been fine."

"No, she couldn't handle you having an affair."

"I didn't have an affair. I didn't even meet Rachel until months after I moved out. We fought all the time about money, my job, well, just about everything. It was bad for both of us."

"That's not the way I remember it."

"I didn't know it was so hard on you. I love you and have never stopped. I just thought you took your mother's side."

"It never was about taking sides. I thought you didn't care about me anymore. Mom was the one who was there. She was the one who cried every night. You went on without us, to Rachel."

Brian stared as his daughter fought her tears. Finally, he got up put her arms around her. "I always cared and always will. I never meant for you to feel that Rachel was more important than you. You and Michael are the best part of my life. I'm proud of who you are and what you've accomplished. I love you, Meggie."

Meg couldn't hold her tears back and threw her arms around her father. "I love you too, Daddy." She clung to her father until her tears subsided. He patted her back and just waited, not knowing what to say.

Brian cleared his throat as Meg dried her tears on a tissue. "What do we do now?" he asked.

"I was trying to follow Grant's movements after he broke out of prison to see where he might be staying. The car he stole was found in the city. I was checking public transportation to see if anyone fitting his description came up to our area."

"I think we ought to leave this to the Marshals."

"I get it. You can leave too, if you want." Meg was sullen.

"I'm not leaving again. I'll stick by your side until either you're ready to go the police or until we get Grant."

"Okay, I do work better with a partner," she said with a little smile.

"Sounds like a plan. Show me what you found."

CHAPTER 25

The dispatcher put the frantic call from Mr. Mendoza through to Reggie, who flew across town to their house. The U.S. Marshals were already en route to pick up Sam and the Mendozas to put them in protective custody. Reggie was furious with Greg Matthews and wondered how the boys could have gotten out.

Reggie pulled up in front of the house to see Mr. Mendoza pacing in the driveway. Greg was nervously standing by the garage as two uniformed officers pulled up in front of the house. As Reggie got out of his car, he pointed the officers toward Greg while he walked over to Mr. Mendoza.

"Captain Bennett, both boys are missing. My wife called me to tell me the boys were gone. I talked to my son over an hour ago and they were supposed to be on their way back. They still aren't back, and Johnny isn't answering his cell phone."

"Are the boys together?" Reggie asked.

"I believe so. They left in Sam's car. They should have been back by now."

"Let's take this one thing at a time. Does Officer Matthews have a description of Sam's car?"

"Yes, I don't know the license plate number, though. I believe it is registered to his father. His father! What will I say to Stanley?"

Reggie turned to one of the officers. "Call in an APB on Sam's car. Get dispatch to get the tag numbers. Ask the state police to put up some roadblocks. Matthews, stay put. I've got some questions for you." He turned back to Mr. Mendoza. "Were you here when the boys left?"

"No, I was at work. But my wife was here."

"Okay, let's go in the house so I can talk to her about what happened."

Mrs. Mendoza was in the kitchen looking nervous. She sat down with her husband at the table. Mrs. Mendoza told Reggie about having coffee with Officer Greg when they realized the boys were gone.

"How long were they gone before you noticed?" Reggie asked.

"It must have been an hour or so," she replied. "I never thought our Johnny would do anything like this."

"Can I see the boys' room?" Reggie asked Mr. Mendoza. Mr. Mendoza led Reggie to Johnny's bedroom. Reggie slipped on some latex gloves and looked through the desk and dresser. He found Sam's bag under the cot and searched it.

Leaving Mr. Mendoza, Reggie called the station to get more police involved in searching for clues. It was getting late in the day, and he wanted to use what daylight remained to find the boys. Cornering Greg in the backyard, Reggie asked him what happened, than blasted him for his incompetence. As word spread through Granelle about the missing boys, neighbors began to show up at the Mendozas'. Reggie sent Greg home to await further disciplinary action.

Reggie waited for him to drive away, then went back in the house to talk to the Mendozas. He found Mrs. Mendoza on the phone telling someone that the boys were missing.

Reggie motioned for her attention. Putting the phone down, Reggie said, "We need to contain this to Granelle. I want to make sure the media doesn't get hold of this story yet."

"I'm trying to see if any of our friends have seen the boys."

"I understand. But I don't want the press to get this story because I don't want Grant to know that Sam is in Granelle."

"I didn't think about that." She quickly ended the conversation.

"Captain Bennett," Mr. Mendoza said. "I had my wife call her mother. I want to send Katie to her grandmother's house in Syracuse."

"I understand your concern for your daughter. But it's probably best to wait until the Marshals get here. Then you, your wife, and daughter can still go to the safe house. Your house is probably going to be very busy most of the night."

"I want my family safe. But I have no plans on leaving Granelle until I know my son and Sam are safe."

"We'll see about that when the Marshals arrive."

"I trusted you earlier and left my family here with one of your officers. Now the boys are missing. If you think you can send me off someplace to just wait while a convicted murderer is looking for Sam, you're wrong."

"I know you keep thinking about little Sam Craig when you talk about the boy. But that kid is nothing but trouble. He's not your son's best friend anymore."

"You're wrong about him, Captain Bennett. Over the past few days, I've seen in Sam as the child he was before his mother was killed. A kid who needs a second chance, someone to believe in him."

"I guarantee you that this whole sneaking away thing was Sam's idea. And if something does happen to the boys, to Johnny, you'll have Sam Craig to thank for that. Not me, not my officer, but that kid you think can be redeemed."

"That boy has done nothing to deserve your distrust."

"Excuse me, Captain," one of the officers interrupted. "The Marshals just arrived and want to talk to you."

"We'll finish this later," Reggie said, turning away.

"No, Captain Bennett, I think we are through talking about this. We won't agree on Sam. If the Marshals want to take my wife and daughter to the safe house, that's fine. But I'm staying until the boys are back safe."

"Okay, for now. But if you get in the way of the investigation, I'll personally take you into protective custody." Reggie walked away before Mr. Mendoza could reply. Reggie went into the backyard where small groups were beginning to search the woods in back of the house. He discussed the situation with the Marshals. They went into the house to try to convince Mr. Mendoza to leave, and Reggie walked to the tree house.

Reggie saw a coffee can full of cigarette butts and looked up the ladder. He saw that the forensic team had already searched the tree house, and he headed toward the woods.

"Captain," someone called out to him from the woods. "I think we found something." Reggie hurried into the woods and up the embankment. At the top of the knoll, an officer stood holding a duffel bag.

"The name tag says 'Sam Craig,'" he said, looking inside. "And look at these footprints. It clearly shows some kind of a struggle."

One team deeper into the woods called out to Reggie too. He went over to them and looked down at the large footprints in the dirt. He recognized them as the same prints from the Petersons' backyard.

The creature stood at the side of the road as if waiting for Sam. Sam slowed the car and felt his heart beginning to pound. Now that he was actually near the creature, Sam felt timid and scared. The dirt road was isolated and no houses could be seen. Sam opened the car door, walked over to the creature, and knelt down on the leaf-covered ground and stared. The creature was just as he remembered. It had a wolf-like appearance, but it was very large. Its eyes were brownish with a dim red glow in the overcast woods. Sam remembered that it had rows of sharp teeth. He looked down at the scar on his finger where the creature had bitten it years ago.

Sam looked back at the creature and held his hand out toward it. "Do you remember this?" The creature lifted its head and took a step toward Sam. Every instinct in Sam told him to run, but he sat still, waiting to see what the creature would do.

It took a few steps toward Sam and then sat down. "I don't understand any of this," Sam whispered. "I feel like I belong with you, and yet I'm scared. Am I the keeper?"

The creature got up and walked to Sam; it wagged its tail a little. Sam reached out, and the creature licked his hand. "They want to take me away. It's because of Trevor."

Suddenly, the creature was alert. It looked in the woods behind him and then back at Sam. It growled low in its throat. Sam jumped up and ran back toward the car. He quickly got in and slammed the door. He could see the creature rushing away deeper into the woods.

Sam sat watching and willing himself to calm down. He had to figure this out. Something else was in the woods, and he felt like the creature warned him. Looking in the rearview mirror, Sam saw how terrified he looked. Yet he felt he had nothing to fear from the creature. Sam didn't wait to find out what the creature was warning him about; he threw the car into gear and drove away.

Sam drove through the back roads until he reached Dunning Road. He sat at the end of the road, afraid to drive to the old Hanson house. He wondered if that was where Trevor was hiding out. He had been thinking for days about Trevor and had practically convinced himself that Trevor wouldn't go there because it would be the most obvious place the police would look. Still, it scared Sam to think about going back to that house.

Sam was about to drive away when he saw the creature step out of the woods. It started walking toward the house and turned to look back at Sam, as if beckoning him to come. Without thinking more about it, Sam turned down Dunning and headed to the old house. The creature raced on ahead of Sam. As he passed his childhood home, Sam didn't even glance at it.

Dusk was beginning to fall, and Sam turned on the headlights on the tree-shrouded road. They briefly illuminated the old house, and the childhood stories that Sam remembered of the house being haunted quickly came to mind. The creature stood toward the back of the house, and Sam pulled the car up the short dirt driveway.

Sam got out to open the door to the old garage. Age and neglect had rusted the hinges and the tall weeds in front of the door made it almost impossible for Sam to pull it open. He stopped and looked at the weeds, realizing that pulling on the door was going to break the weeds. It would be a dead giveaway that the garage was being used. Instead, he went back to his car and drove it into the backyard.

The woods had taken over most of the yard, and Sam pulled far back into the tangle of weeds. He took some leaves and branches and put them on his car to conceal it. He looked around and saw the creature waiting for him on the back porch. Sam went over to him, and they looked at each other.

"I remember seeing you down at my house in Poughkeepsie. You stayed with me all these years, so I guess that means I'm safe with you and that I am the keeper. But I don't know what that means or what I'm supposed to do."

The creature sat listening and then got up and pawed at the door. "Hey, I don't want to go inside." The creature came back to Sam and then walked back to the door, pawing at it again. Sam got up and took down the old police tape. He opened the door and the creature went inside. When Sam didn't follow, the creature came out, pawed Sam, and then went back inside, turning to see if Sam would follow. Still Sam just stood, afraid to go into the house.

"Okay," Sam finally said. It was pitch black inside the house. The creature went deeper inside, but it was too dark for Sam to see. The creature's eyes glowed deep red, and it came back to see why Sam had stopped. He barked and Sam said, "I can't see. It's too dark in here for me."

It came back and pulled at Sam's T-shirt with its teeth. Sam remembered how sharp the teeth were and let himself be guided through the kitchen. Sam knew the layout of the house from when he and Johnny had snooped around when they were kids. He knew the doorway that he was led to went to the basement.

"Please, I don't want to go down there." But the creature pawed the door, making scratches in the wood. Sam opened the door and it went down the steps. It barked back up to Sam. Sam relented and felt for the first step. His hand brushed cobwebs and he shuddered. Keeping his hand on the cement wall, Sam carefully took each step in the darkness. The creature watched from the bottom of the steps. Sam knew that there were little rooms in the basement, the rooms where Trevor had kept the women he had abducted all those years ago. Sam stood at the bottom of the steps, not knowing what to do. The creature had gone ahead into the interior rooms in the basement.

Finally Sam felt his way into the room with the cage. He remembered the workbench against the wall. He felt around until he found a candle. As he took his lighter out to light the candle, Sam laughed at himself. Sam lit the candle and it illuminated the small room. The creature looked up at him and cocked its head. "I didn't need the candle. I could have used the lighter to see," Sam explained to the creature. "I'm an idiot sometimes."

Sam's moment of levity was gone as he turned and looked around the room. He remembered this room so well, where he had been held a prisoner. With mounting dread, Sam stared at the cage. Cobwebs hung from the ceiling and thick dust covered everything. The old blanket Sam had used all those years before still lay in a heap in the middle of the cage.

The creature made a low sound and Sam looked toward it. It was heading down a hallway past the rooms and the cage. Sam followed the creature, and the candlelight cast wavy shadows in the room. Down the hall was a deep interior room. The boxes had been sorted through years before, but most of everything had just been abandoned by the police after the investigation.

Sam began to look inside of boxes to see what they contained. Clothes, blankets, old food, much of which had deteriorated over time. In one of the boxes of clothes, Sam found mice and dropped the box. The mice scattered, running into crevices in the walls. The creature lay watching as Sam began to take the least soiled blankets and put them on the floor. Once Sam had a thick bedding of blankets, he laid on the floor. The creature laid his head on Sam's legs, and Sam was soon asleep.

CHAPTER 26

The take-out cartons from the Chinese restaurant were empty. Meg stretched as she stood to turn on the lights. Night was falling and she felt no closer to the missing pieces that would lead to Grant. But she finally felt safe. She stood in the doorway watching her father trying to do a search on the Internet and smiled. Brian's cell phone rang and he answered it.

"I didn't realize it was this late," Brian said, looking at his watch and then Meg. "Soon. I'll just wrap up what I'm working on and then come home...yeah, Meg's still here too...I'll ask, but...well, no guarantees. See you soon."

Brian snapped the phone closed. "Didn't realize how late it's getting. Rachel wondered if you'd come stay at our place tonight."

"I think I'll probably just stay here tonight. I want to get to Granelle at first light. He's got to be somewhere close."

"I don't want you going to Granelle without me. We're partners now, remember?"

"Then maybe you ought to stay too."

"Hey, I'm too old to be sleeping on a love seat," he said as his cell phone rang again. "Hello...yeah...what happened...where's Bennett? Okay...thanks for the heads up... I know I owe you big time."

"What happened?"

"It's not good news. The boys are missing. The Marshals were on their way to get the family and the boys snuck out. They were on their way back to the house and it looks like they disappeared."

"What does this mean? Do they think Grant kidnapped them?"

"My buddy doesn't have a lot of info yet. He's going to see what's going on and call me back. But I think you're right about going to Granelle. Maybe we should head over there tonight."

"Sounds like a good idea to me. You'd better call Rachel and let her know."

"Yeah, but I'm not sure you're really going to like my idea."

"Why? We're going to help look for the boys...aren't we?"

"No, I think we ought to go get Jake."

"He made it clear that he didn't want to be involved anymore. And frankly, I don't want him around either."

"If we're going rogue, we need some backup."

"We have each other. We don't need Jake."

"Sure we do. I've got a feeling about something and I think we need Jake to draw out Grant."

"I'm not following you." Meg flopped down in the love seat.

"I've been looking at all this stuff on the Internet about the legend. It was all that information you found out six years ago that Bennett said was hogwash."

"Let's not get back into that stuff. That ruined my police career."

"But it's the key to finding Grant. I was reading all of the police reports and news articles from Grant's arrest. Remember, he needs four women to be sacrificed in exchange for the rights of being the keeper. That's what he wants, because he believes it is his legacy."

"What does that have to do with Jake?"

"That Shamus O'Leary guy said in one of his statements that the praying minister was the one that ruined it before. It wasn't that Jake solved the case, but that he prayed."

"So you want to go ask Jake to pray?"

"Couldn't hurt, but no. I want Grant to see Jake as front and center. If Grant believes what O'Leary said about the power Jake possesses in his prayers, it might draw him out. He might make a mistake and try to get Jake out of the way, to stop him from ruining his plan again."

"But Grant taking Jake's wife was personal. To hurt Jake."

"Because he probably thought he could scare Jake into sitting back and doing nothing. If Grant sees Jake in either role, cop or preacher, coming after him, he's going to go after Jake, and we'll be right there to nab him."

"Look, Dad, I had no problem with Jake helping us, but I don't want to use him as bait anymore than I want to use Sam."

"Do you have a better plan?"

"No, but I know Jake, and he's not going to agree to helping us."

"Let's go find out."

"Wait, Dad. There's something that I never told anyone. I didn't want to get into this, but since you brought it up..." Meg started, but then stopped. She looked at Brian and then plunged ahead. "I never said anything to anyone. It seemed so bizarre back when I was investigating the case. Everyone thought I was crazy as it was."

"What is it, Meg?"

"That creature's DNA. The lab reports all confirmed it, but no one said anything. That creature has human DNA mixed in with animal DNA."

"Human?"

"I just thought someone faked the analysis to make the old myth about it being part werewolf true. But our reports showed the same DNA strain."

"Did Bennett know this?"

"He never wanted to talk about the creature, so I doubt it."

"Well, let's go talk to Jake."

"Okay, but Dad, don't mention this to him. I think it would make him not want to help."

Jake was restless and found it hard to do anything. Darkness had fallen on Granelle, and Jake knew it would be a long time before he fell asleep. As he ate a cold sandwich for dinner, he got out his Bible and read Psalm 61. "Hear my cry, O God; listen to my prayer. From the ends of the earth I call to you, I call as my heart grows faint; lead me to the rock that is higher than I." The words spoke to him and he sat reading.

Jake turned from the mess in the kitchen and went outside. The evening sky was overcast and hazy, offering no relief from the heat of the day. Jake sat in the lawn chair and stared into the dark woods. He thought about that creature watching his house and wondered if it was still out there somewhere.

Jake heard Buddy whining at the door and got up to let him out. The dog sniffed around the backyard, but didn't react to anything. The dog finally came over to Jake and lay down near the chair. Jake let his thoughts drift back over the past few days since Sarah had disappeared. He had made a lot of rash decisions. He didn't regret finding Doug and stopping him from committing suicide, even though it had alienated him from Reggie. It had been worth saving his life.

A car pulled in the driveway, and Buddy ran, barking, to side of the house. Jake followed him. Buddy was jumping around the car as Brian and Meg got out.

Brian took the lead and walked up to Jake. "We thought we should come and talk things out with you. Can we come in?"

Jake shrugged and they went into the house. Once in the living room, Brian began again. "Have you heard about the boys?"

"I haven't heard anything. I've been here alone since I left you guys."

"Sam Craig was staying with the Mendozas. Now Sam and Johnny are missing."

"Johnny Mendoza? The Mendozas are members of my church," Jake said. "What happened?"

"Apparently, Grant was seen in Saratoga, so the U.S. Marshals were coming to take the family and Sam to a safe house. The boys snuck out of the house and never came back."

"Did they run away? Or do they think Trevor got them?"

"I don't know yet. My friend is going to call me once he gets more information."

"I probably should call the family and see if there is anything I can do," Jake said absent-mindedly.

Brian and Meg exchanged glances. "Actually, I have an idea that might resolve everything. I was thinking that you, me, and Meg should join the search for the boys in the morning."

"Of course, I'll help in the search. So many people were helping look for Sarah."

"I don't mean like join a search team. I mean we make it clear to everyone we are a part of the investigation, not just the search."

Jake looked from Brian to Meg and then shook his head. "No. I don't know where you're going with this. But I won't do anything to jeopardize Sarah's life."

"You won't be," Meg said, taking over. "Remember, it takes four women to complete the blood ritual. Sarah's only one. He won't do anything until he has three more, and one will have to be me."

"This is personal, Meg. He took Sarah to hurt me."

"You were there in that basement when Sam declared he was the keeper. You saw that creature turn on Trevor. Dad found out that Shamus O'Leary is dead. Do you think it's a coincidence that the creature is here in Granelle? It's here because Sam Craig is here, and he's the keeper. Trevor wants that right; he thinks it was his birthright."

"Then why Sarah?"

"Because you're right about it being personal. The two people he wants to hurt most are you and me. And to hurt you, he makes Sarah victim number one."

"But what about the boys?"

"I figure Sam's on the run. He's scared about Grant and just takes off with his best friend. But if Grant gets him, Sam's dead for sure. He stole his legacy."

"I still think we should talk this over with Reggie."

"We will," Brian said before Meg could answer. "But in the morning. Let's strategize tonight and make a plan. Is it all right if we bunk down here tonight? I'm not a fan of Meggie's love seat."

"I've got a guest room you can use. You'll just have to get the dog to make room on the bed."

"Sounds fine. Let's get busy figuring out where to start in the morning."

"We start with Reggie or I'm out," Jake said, looking between them. Meg and Brian exchanged glances again and then Meg nodded.

"I'll put on some coffee. I know I need it," Brian headed to the kitchen.

CHAPTER 27

Sam woke up in the basement alone. At first, he felt like he was eleven again and he was immediately awake. But he wasn't locked in the cage. He wondered where the creature was and what he was going to eat. Wishing he had thought about food last night, he got up and began to think about what he was going to do now. Sam had very little money and even fewer options. He knew going to his house in Poughkeepsie would be a mistake, and he couldn't turn to Karen or his aunt either. Although he realized it was probably a bad idea to leave the Mendozas' house, Sam did feel like this was the best decision for keeping them safe.

With a little outside light coming through the small basement window, Sam began to look through the boxes again. Hoping he wouldn't find any more mice, he sifted through the belongings that Trevor and Shamus had left behind years ago. Mostly Sam found old clothes and blankets. There were some old tools and stuff Sam didn't recognize. In the bottom box, Sam found some books and a leather satchel that was stuck between them.

Sam pulled the satchel out and opened it up. Inside were two leather-bound books. Sam opened one to find it was a handwritten journal. It was written in a language Sam didn't know. He wondered if he could figure out what some of the words were on the Internet. Sam sat back on the blankets and flipped through the journals. He sighed, feeling very hungry. Thinking he might find a candy bar somewhere in his car, Sam got up, taking the satchel that contained the journals with him.

Sam walked back upstairs without pausing in the chamber where he had been held. Upstairs, light poured in all the windows. The creature was lying in the kitchen near the back door. He got up when Sam came in and pawed at the door. Sam let it out of the house and went into the backyard toward his car. The creature took off for the woods, not paying attention to Sam. Sam took his keys out of his pocket and unlocked his trunk. He found an old candy bar and a crushed half-empty bag of chips mixed in with a bunch of junk. It was better than nothing. He put the satchel in the car and closed the trunk.

Sam knew that for now, he needed to just stay at the house. He didn't want anyone to find him. He felt foolish for staying in Granelle now that it was morning. His curiosity about the creature, though, had kept him here. Once it was dark, Sam planned on getting out of town. He didn't know of anyone whom he could turn to. Sam thought about getting his cell phone of out the car, but what did it matter? The only ones who would be trying to get him would be the Mendozas.

Sam went back in the house and turned on the water in the kitchen. The faucet gurgled and then stopped. It was already hot and Sam really wanted a drink. He looked through the cupboard to find filthy dishes. There were some old canned goods, and boxes that had already been chewed and left by the mice. Sam opened the old refrigerator to find unrecognizable rotten food. Closing the door in frustration, Sam left the kitchen and looked around the old house.

In an old broom closet under the steps, Sam found packaging that once was a case of bottled water. There was one bottle left and Sam eagerly grabbed it. Using his shirt, Sam wiped off the dust that had accumulated on the bottle. He opened it and took a long drink. It tasted weird, but that was okay with Sam. He put the bottle aside and dug into the candy bar. While he ate, Sam wandered through the old rooms. He remembered the old furniture and pictures that had belonged to Mr. Hanson. He wondered who owned the house now that it had been left for so long.

Sam finally sat in one of the dusty old chairs in the living room. The heat permeated the house. He sat for a while thinking about what he was going to do, where he could go, how he would pay for anything. Certainly, the police were looking for him, and Trevor definitely was looking for him. What was he going to do? For the first time, Sam wished his father was back and he could just go home, letting his father worry about all this. He thought about going back to the Mendozas and again decided not to let them risk their lives for him.

Sam's meager food and water were gone. The humidity crushed him and he wanted to get out of the house. Going back out through the kitchen, Sam stepped into the backyard again. The heat was as bad outside and he looked at the woods, knowing it would be a little cooler under the dense trees. He longed for the old caves from his childhood. It would be really cool there inside the rock walls. Maybe he'd even find the old cans of soda he left in there so many years before.

The interior of the woods was cooler, but the humidity hung heavy in the air. It felt good to be outside, alone for a change. He walked in the woods to the back of what was his old house. He stopped, looking at the changes that the new owners had made. Realizing their car wasn't in the driveway, Sam crept into the yard. He peeked into the kitchen window and was surprised that it was remodeled. It wasn't his old house anymore. He turned to go back to the woods and saw the hose coiled up next to the back steps.

Sam turned on the water and waited for a minute until the water turned cold. He took a long drink from the hose. Refreshed, Sam shut off the water and then decided to see if the house was unlocked. Turning the handle, he found it was locked, but noticed the window over the kitchen sink was opened a little. He took a lawn chair and stood on it, then popped the screen out and opened the window further. Sam pulled himself up and through the window. He fell into the sink, but it was empty. He laughed at himself, excited by what he was doing. Sam had never broken into a house, but he felt a sense of belonging to this house. It was the first place he ever lived. Getting off the counter, Sam turned to the refrigerator. He found leftover pizza and ate it cold.

Taking the pizza with him, Sam went upstairs to his old bedroom. Disappointment washed over him when he saw it had been turned into a girl's room. The ballerinas on the bedspread and curtains matched the ballerina picture on the pink wall. Feeling guilty and suddenly nervous, Sam dashed back downstairs. He found a large bottle of soda in the kitchen and took it with him. He let himself out the door and relockedit.. He looked up at the window and realized that locking the door wouldn't matter. He couldn't put the screen back in now, so he stepped back on the lawn chair to close the window.

Sam went back to the woods, the pizza sitting heavy in his stomach. He couldn't wait to get to the caves now. He thought about his car and still planned to leave Granelle tonight once it was dark. When Sam got near the caves wall, he heard voices. He froze and ducked down behind a tree. Sam looked up to the cave he had once claimed for himself. If he could climb up there without being seen, he thought he'd be safe.

Sam strained to hear what the voices were saying, but it was too far away and muffled. Whoever was talking was in one of the lower caves. Looking back up the rock wall, a movement caught Sam's eye. He looked toward the largest cave, the cave he suddenly remembered Trevor taking him to when he was abducted. Sam was startled to see the creature staring right at him near the mouth of the cave.

The creature turned its attention back to the cave. Sam heard voices again and knew he had to see who was talking. He crept through the woods closer to the large cave, being careful to stay hidden in the deep foliage and behind trees. The voices were clearer, and he recognized one of them as Trevor's.

Sam froze, too terrified to move. There was a soft voice answering Trevor. While Sam wanted to know what was going on, he also wanted to run for his life. He saw the creature looking around to see where Sam was. Sam felt betrayed by the creature. He slowed his breathing so he could hold himself very still. The creature didn't see him, but sat and sniffed the air. Then, it looked directly at Sam.

"Come," Trevor said, leaving the cave. "That boy is around here some-place."

Sam stared at Trevor. He was just as Sam remembered him with dark black hair and eyes. His olive complexion had turned to a deep bronze from the sun. He looked around, and Sam froze as his eyes swept right where Sam was hiding in the bushes.

The creature turned and followed Trevor, glancing back at Sam. Sam crouched behind the tree for a long time, afraid any movement would give him away. He couldn't help wondering if the person in the cave was Mrs. Peterson. If it was, Sam knew he couldn't just leave her there. He remembered what it felt like to be Trevor's prisoner, and Pastor Jake had been so nice to Sam when he was a kid.

Figuring he had a little time, Sam finally got up and slowly moved toward the cave. There was no place to hide close to the rock wall. But Sam had to see who was in there talking to Trevor. He dashed toward the cave and peaked inside. It was dark, and Sam stepped into the coolness. As his eyes adjusted to the dim interior, Sam saw an old cage. It was just like the one in the basement of the Hanson house. He crept closer, realizing that two people were in the cage. One person was lying on an old blanket and the other was sitting up with his back to Sam.

Sam's sneaker made a scraping sound on the rocks and the person turned. Gasping, Sam rushed to the cage. "Johnny? What are you doing here?" Sam asked in a frantic whisper.

"After you left, I decided to cut through the woods to go home, but Trevor was there watching our house," Johnny whispered back. "He's looking for you. He wants to kill you."

"Is that Mrs. Peterson?" Sam asked, nodding toward the woman.

"Yeah, she's been asleep the whole time. Get us out of here!"

"Okay. Where'd Trevor put the key?" Sam looked around the cave. There was a rock ledge that held a lantern and a few other items. But Sam didn't see a key.

"It's in his pocket with my cell phone," Johnny said flatly. "There isn't anything over there that you can use to break the lock?"

"Not really. Just rope, matches, other junk." Sam felt around on the ground until he found a large rock. "Get back. Let me see if I can break the padlock with this." Sam hit the padlock a bunch of times with the rock, but he couldn't break it.

"Sam, stop. It's making too much noise. If Trevor hears it, he'll just come back and then you'll get caught. Just hurry and get some help."

"Okay," Sam said and then hesitated. "I'm sorry that you're here. I thought if I left, he'd leave your family alone."

"Can we talk about this later? I'm afraid."

"Yeah," Sam turned. He got to the entrance of the cave and glanced around. The caves were deep in the woods near the desolate part of town. Sam knew the fastest way to get help would be to go back to the Hanson house and get his car. He dashed back into the comfort of the woods, very much aware that Trevor was also in the woods looking for him.

CHAPTER 28

Jake found it hard to sleep with Brian snoring across the hall. Finally, as the sky was just turning gray, he gave up and got dressed. Meg was already up, drinking a cup of coffee.

"I thought you'd still be asleep," Jake said getting a mug out of the cupboard.

"Who can sleep with Dad snoring?" Meg said with a grin. Buddy was curled up next to Meg's chair, and Felix was on her lap. As Jake sat with the coffee, Brian walked in, ready for the day.

"Well, we better get moving. You both ready to head out?" Brian asked. Meg pushed the cat off her lap and got up.

"Not yet," Jake said, getting up too. "I want to call Reggie first."

"Why don't we just stop at the station on our way?" Brian glanced over at Meg. This time Jake saw the look and shook his head.

"No. I want to let Reggie know what we know."

Jake went into the other room to make the call. Brian trailed after him. Jake talked to the dispatcher and found that Reggie was out on a new case and not available. Jake gave her his cell number and asked her to relay an urgent message to him.

"All right, I tried. I just can't sit still any longer. Let's see if we can find Reggie. Granelle is small enough that he should be easy to find," Jake said, looking at Brian for support.

"Sure. Meg, let's go," Brian called out.

Jake followed them out to the car, feeling uneasy. The drive was quiet and Jake began to pray for wisdom. As they passed the old Craig house, Jake realized where they were headed. Dunning Road was quiet and desolate in the early morning. The few houses were empty, and the drive to the deserted old house seemed long. Jake sat in the backseat looking at the old house as Meg and Brian got out of the car.

"Aren't you coming?" Brian asked Jake.

"No, I'll wait. Reggie won't be here. He already checked this lead out a few days ago when Sarah went missing."

Meg waited for Brian to catch up and they disappeared behind the house. They were gone for a while and Jake got hot sitting in the car. Finally, he got out and began to walk to the house.

As Jake reached the back, Brian met him. "Jake," he began. "We found Sam's car. He hasn't been abducted. It looks like he spent the night here. There are footprints in the dust at the house that show the creature was here too. It's just possible that we have this all wrong. What if Sam is working with Trevor, and this is all about revenge?"

"What do you mean?"

"Just that. We've already asked the question about coincidence. How is it possible that Sam is here when Grant is looking for him? Sam is with that creature." Brian paused. "Did you make any headway on that letter Grant got in prison?"

Jake shook his head. "No. Doug said his letter was from O'Leary, and that he had died. Doug doesn't remember a lot of the content. I haven't found out who the attorney is that sent the letters."

"So, we don't know who that letter was from that Grant received. What if it was from Sam? He comes back here, lets Grant know he's in place. What if Sam took Sarah?"

"But that makes no sense. Grant called me asking me for Sam in exchange for Sarah."

"Look, Jake. All I know is that Sam's car is here and he is with that animal. No one has found Sarah yet. We need to follow Sam into the woods. If we do that, maybe we find Sarah."

Meg stood behind her father not saying anything. She knew the only way to get Jake to go with them was for her father to talk him into it. With him talking so much about finding Sarah, she could tell Jake was coming around.

Brian pressed him. "Let's just try this. If we don't find anything, we can go to the station together, all three of us, and report what we know to Bennett. But we can't let this opportunity slip away. Bennett has to be up at the Mendoza place searching for the boys. He won't leave that scene to come here if he's already exhausted this lead. He feels that ground has already been covered. I'm afraid if we miss this opportunity...."

Jake silently prayed for wisdom. He strongly felt Meg shouldn't go into the woods. "Why can't we just wait until Reggie is free?"

"I'm not waiting any longer," Meg said. "I'm going into those woods with or without you."

"I told you the other day that you shouldn't go into the woods. I still feel really strongly right now that you shouldn't go."

Meg shook her head. "If we wait, we lose this fresh lead. Do you really think Bennett is going to listen to me, of all people? He just doesn't like me. I'm sorry about the way I was before. But I really don't want anything to happen to Sarah. Please, Jake, come with us. Help us finish this."

They stood looking at each other for a long moment. Then Meg turned and walked toward the woods. Brian watched her go. "Well, I'd better follow. Don't want her taking off without me. I just feel like you need to be with us, Jake. Can't shake that feeling."

"Brian, promise me this: we just gather evidence and see where the trail goes. Once we get anything solid, we go to Bennett."

"Absolutely," Brian said, "but we'd better get moving. Hold on a minute, Meg."

Meg waited while Brian ran back to the car. He opened his glove box, took out a gun, and handed it to Jake.

Jake waved it away, "Brian, I can't take that. I'm not licensed to carry a weapon."

"What if we run into that creature or Grant? Be safe." Jake stared at the gun for a few long moments. Meg started walking again. "Look, you probably won't even need it. But if you do, I don't want to have to hand it to you then. It's registered to me."

As Meg disappeared behind the house, Jake took the gun. He felt the weight of it in his hand and then stuck it into his waistband. Somehow having the gun made him feel a little safer.

CHAPTER 29

Sam barely glanced at his old house as he snuck through the woods. Thirsty, he couldn't help thinking of the bottle of soda he abandoned near the caves. He stopped as he heard noises in the woods. Crouching down, he looked around and inched forward. Sam kept moving, staying low so he could hide behind rocks and trees. It was a long stretch between the last of the houses and the dead end where the old Hanson house sat.

Sam heard a tree branch snap. His heart was pounding and he froze. He heard the noise again from just to his left. Glancing over, he saw the creature a few hundred feet from him. Moving cautiously through the woods just ahead of the creature was Trevor. Sam realized with panic that Trevor was heading toward the Hanson house. Once there, he would find Sam's car, and he wouldn't be able to get help for Johnny.

Sam thought that if he waited until Trevor was ahead of him, he could double back to his old house. The creature suddenly turned and looked directly at Sam, and then at Trevor. Sam crouched down lower into the thick foliage. He kept his eyes on Trevor. Suddenly Trevor hid and the creature was alert. Sam heard voices coming from the direction of the Hanson house.

Sam wanted to jump out and warn whoever it was, but he was terrified. He glanced over to where the creature and Trevor were and didn't see them. The voices became clearer, and Sam could hear them getting closer. Suddenly, the creature jumped out and ran toward the voices.

"No!" Trevor shouted. The voices became excited. Sam saw Trevor run toward the voices too. He froze for only a moment then fled in the other direction.

Meg, Jake, and Brian were fanned out and walking toward Trevor and the creature. The sight of the creature rushing at them surprised them all. It lunged at Brian, knocking him off his feet backward, while growling and attacking. Meg screamed and ran toward her father.

Brian was yelling, trying to protect himself. Meg pulled out her gun as she ran. She pointed it at the creature and didn't see Trevor running at her.

As she pulled the trigger, Trevor got between them and the bullet hit him. He was knocked off his feet by the impact. The creature turned, blood dripping from its muzzle. It saw Trevor fall and the woman rushing at him. Narrowing its eyes, it turned on Meg. Another gunshot sounded, and this bullet hit the creature. It yowled in agony and took off deep into the woods.

Meg fell on the ground next to her father. She cried as she looked at the bite marks on his neck and shoulders. "No, no," she murmured. She ripped the bottom of her shirt. With shaking hands, she quickly pressed it against the wounds on her father.

Brian looked up into Meg's eyes. He tried to say something. "Daddy, don't, please," Meg sobbed.

Jake ran over to where Trevor had fallen, pulled out his cell phone and dialed 911. No one saw Sam as he disappeared deeper into the woods.

Brian closed his eyes. "Daddy, stay with me. Do you hear me? I can't lose you now," Meg kept crying, and she laid her head on her father's chest.

Jake fell to his knees on the ground next to them. "Meg, Trevor's dead."

"What?" Meg looked up at him, tears still streaming down her face.

"I didn't get to ask him where Sarah is. How will we find Sarah now?" Jake asked. He looked down at Brian and picked up his wrist, checking his pulse. He saw the blood that Brian was quickly losing. Jake pulled off his T-shirt and folded it into a tourniquet. He moved Meg's hands.

"No, Jake," Meg said, pushing at Jake's hand.

"Meg, go out to the road so the ambulance can find us," Jake said, firmly taking over.

"I'm not leaving him," Meg said.

"If you don't go to the road, they will never find us here. Your father could die." Jake knew he was hurting her, but needed to get her to listen. "Go, I can hear the siren. Don't let them miss us."

Meg nodded and quickly got to her feet. She turned back around. "Jake, please don't let my dad die." Then she turned and ran for the road.

With all the blood from her father on her clothes, Meg had a hard time convincing the EMTs that she was fine and to get into the woods to help her father. Reggie pulled up in his car as Meg and the EMTs ran back into the woods. Following them, Reggie glared at Jake as he knelt beside the wounded man.

Jake stepped back as the paramedics began to work on Brian. One ran back to the ambulance for plasma while the other held pressure on the wounds. As the paramedic came back, Jake motioned to Reggie to follow him to where

Trevor lay. Meg knelt by her father's feet crying and watching everything that was being done for him.

Jake watched while Reggie checked Trevor's vitals and called the station to have the coroner come for the body.

Jake hung his head. Reggie glared at him. "What is going on here, Peterson?" Reggie was seething.

"We found Sam Craig's car at the old Hanson house and decided to see what he was doing. I don't know what we were thinking. We just acted on instinct."

"Is that your story?"

"Does it matter now? Trevor's dead, the only person who knows where Sarah is. Reggie, what have I done?" Jake sank down in the deep foliage near Trevor. Anger swept over him, and Jake grabbed Trevor by his shirt. He screamed at him. "What did you do with her? Where is my wife?"

"Jake, stop," Reggie shouted, trying to pull Jake away. Jake continued to scream at Trevor until he was overcome with grief. Reggie finally managed to get Jake to let go of Trevor's shirt. He pulled Jake away from the body as an EMT came over to check it.

Meg looked over and watched as Reggie tried to console Jake. Meg had never seen anyone so broken. Another police car came to the scene, and Reggie told them to drive Jake home. Reggie watched with concern as the officer had to lead Jake to the car. He made a brief call and then turned his attention to Meg.

"Okay, Riley, your turn. What happened here?"

"We were running our own investigation. After we heard about the boys missing, we came out this morning to look. It's like Jake said, we found Sam's car at the Hanson place."

Another ambulance pulled up, and they watched in silence as more people flooded the woods. As the paramedics stabilized Brian, a stretcher was brought in and several men carried him out of the woods to the awaiting ambulance. Finally Meg let one the paramedics clean her hands to be sure she wasn't injured. She was climbing into the ambulance with her father when Reggie stopped her.

"I need a full statement from you. I need to know every move you've made over the past few days. There's still missing people and the one who can give us the answers is dead," Reggie said.

"I need to make sure my father is all right first, and then you can yell at me all you want to," she said in a defeated voice. "Nothing will matter if I led my father into the woods to...." Her voice broke.

"Look, Riley, Sarah's been missing for days now. I've got parents worried about their sons. I need answers now, not later," Reggie demanded.

"What we found won't help you find Sarah or the boys. We just stumbled on Grant. We didn't know where to find him. Can I go with my dad?" Meg said in a small voice.

"Fine. But we still need to talk." Reggie nodded to the ambulance driver. Meg climbed in, and it took off with sirens blaring.

After the coroner arrived and declared Trevor deceased, the other ambulance took his body to the medical examiner's office. Reggie was called away from the scene to a break-in down the road, while the forensic team searching the area found Meg's gun. They took it and Jake's gun and put them in evidence bags.

Sam heard the gun shots and ducked down. A few moments later the creature ran past him and into the woods. Sam saw blood on its back flank and followed it. He lost the creature many times as he followed it deep into the woods, but was able to follow the bloody trail. Sam called out to it a couple of times, but it just kept pushing deeper and deeper. He didn't even recognize where he was anymore, but he was driven by an instinct to follow the creature, to protect it.

Finally, Sam found the creature lying on its side, breathing heavily. Its hind end was covered in blood and it growled at Sam as he knelt next to it. Sam tried to pet it, but it snapped at him.

"I don't know what to do," Sam said. "Why did you go so far in? I can't get you help in here."

The creature closed its eyes. Its breathing became harder and more labored. "You did this to save me from Trevor. I thought you were on his side. But you went at them so Trevor wouldn't see me, didn't you," Sam said softly. The creature opened its eyes and looked up at Sam. "You understand me, don't you?"

The creature closed its eyes, took a few shallow breaths and then lay still. "No. Not now. You can't die now!"

Tears streamed down his face, and Sam buried his head in the dirty fur. He cried for a long time saying "no" again and again. But the creature didn't move. Sam cried until he couldn't anymore. Instinctively, he moved away from the creature and began to dig in the dark rich soil with his hands. As he hit rocks, he used one to help him dig. Covered with dirt and sweat, Sam dug a shallow grave. He pulled the creature over to it and buried it. Stumbling away from this place, Sam knew he needed to go back and help Mrs. Peterson and Johnny. Now that the creature was dead, Sam didn't even care if Trevor killed him.

CHAPTER 30

Jake stumbled into his house, emotionally and physically exhausted. He knew he should not have gone into the woods that morning. Deep down, Jake knew that Trevor didn't intend to let Sarah go. What did it matter now? Trevor was dead and Sarah was still lost somewhere, probably drugged and locked up. Buddy met Jake at the door with his tail wagging, and Jake absentmindedly patted the big dog. He went to the living room and sank into the couch. Buddy jumped up next to him and laid his big head on Jake's lap.

Jake turned on the television hoping that it would offer him something to think about besides his failings. He listened for a while as Dennis Miller and Bill O'Reilly discussed the latest problems in Washington, but he just couldn't keep his mind on the show. Another day was passing. Sarah was still gone, Trevor was dead, and Brian was probably in surgery.

Jake had tried to pray, but the words just wouldn't come. How could he turn to God now? Jake wandered around the house with Buddy trailing him. Buddy kept constant vigil, somehow knowing his master was hurting. Jake found himself in the bedroom and sat on his edge of the bed. Buddy jumped up next to him.

The doorbell rang, and Buddy barked and ran downstairs. Jake followed the dog and was surprised to see Walt and Millie at the door.

As Jake opened the door, Walt said, "Reggie Bennett called me and told me he thought you might need your old pastor. I know you weren't expecting us, but Reggie felt you needed us to be here."

"You know you're welcome here anytime," Jake said, reaching down and giving Millie a hug.

"We don't know what's going on with you," Walt said. "But we've been around a long time and know that something's not right beyond Sarah being lost." Walt settled on the couch.

Jake didn't want to tell Walt what he had done, but he hung his head in shame. Millie patted Jake's arm and went into the kitchen to make some tea. Jake sank down in the overstuffed chair in the corner of the little room. The late afternoon sun poured into the windows and Jake looked out toward the woods across the road.

"Jake," Walt began. "I knew on Wednesday that something was wrong. I should have stayed for a few minutes to talk to you."

"I've made some pretty big mistakes in the past few days," Jake began. "I don't know what to do, Walt. Just yesterday morning, I spent time in prayer, felt God leading me to work with Meg, and then I rush ahead and now...."

"We all make mistakes. One of the biggest steps you can take is just admitting you've made them."

"My mistakes may cost Sarah her life," Jake said softly as his eyes filled with tears.

"You have no way of knowing that."

"Trevor's dead. He was shot this morning in the woods near the old Hanson house. If I hadn't gone along with this whole scheme, maybe Reggie could have found Trevor before he was killed." Jake's voice was full of raw emotion. He felt like a condemned man.

"I hate even asking you this, but with the way you're acting, the look on your face...did you shoot Trevor?"

Jake looked up with sadness, "No, but I might as well have. It was Meg, and it was an accident. That creature was attacking her father and she took a shot at it. The bullet hit Trevor instead."

The tea kettle whistled and Millie, listening from the kitchen, breathed a sigh of relief. She was thankful that Jake hadn't been the one to shoot Trevor. She prayed quietly while she gathered the items for tea. Setting the mugs on a tray, she poured hot water into each mug. She carried the tray into the living room and sat next to her husband on the couch.

"Were you all in the woods looking for the boys?" Walt reached for a mug.

"That was our excuse. But I know deep down we were all there hunting for Trevor. I don't understand how I got entangled in this. I just wanted Sarah safe. When I got that call and heard Trevor's voice, my judgment got all messed up. It was wrong. I know that now. But I felt like God was allowing this. How could I have been so wrong when I'm a pastor?"

"Pastors aren't perfect. I should know, I'm married to one," Millie said with a small smile. She blew on her tea and took a small sip. Jake just sat playing with the tea bag, not bothering to even try to drink it. Mille got up and went back to the kitchen. She began cleaning up the days of accumulated dishes. Jake sat lost in thought, not noticing.

After a few moments of silence, Walt said, "Do you remember the verse:

'Two are better than one, because they have a good return for their work: If one falls down, his friend can help him up. But pity the man who falls and has no one to help him up! Though one may be overpowered, two can defend themselves. A cord of three strands is not quickly broken?'"

"Of course, from Ecclesiastes."

"I've been praying for you, Jake. I understand you needed a few days off, but had no idea you were involving yourself in the investigation. Why didn't you come to us?"

"I don't want to involve you in this."

"Seeing that this situation is literally life and death for Sarah, did you ask others to join you in praying for discernment and direction?"

"I didn't think of it," Jake said lamely.

"You are the pastor of the church. This entire church loves Sarah and has been searching for her, bringing you meals, trying any way to help you. We will do everything we can to help you, even now."

"I just didn't know what to do. I had to figure out where Grant was. I need to find Sarah. Reggie won't tell me anything else because I tracked down Doug. Even though I know Doug is innocent in all this, the police were wasting time watching him instead of focusing on Grant."

"Jake I'm not going to sit here condemning you for your choices. I know I've made some shaky choices in my life, too. I and many members of the church are Ecclesiastes-type friends to you. We will be here to support you and help you get through this tough time. What are you going to do now?"

"I don't know. But I keep looking at how Reggie is handling the investigation. I know how to run an investigation, how to find clues, and to hunt down suspects."

"But you never did that work for members of your family. You know that even if you were on the force that you would have to step aside to let others do the work."

"Yes, but Reggie is doing it wrong," Jake said. "He doesn't have all the facts either."

"What facts? Things you found out while doing your own investigation?" Jake hesitated and then looked away. "If you were the investigator, was this information you would have wanted to know?"

"Yeah, but sometimes it leads to the hostage's death. I can't take that risk with Sarah."

"But you weren't the investigator. You left police work to go into ministry. You should trust God with Sarah's life."

"I just don't know what to do now."

"Pastor Jake would know. The pastor who was once the best detective in Saratoga County would know what to say to this man who sits in his office. This former detective who is still good friends with the captain of the police force. What would you say, Pastor Jake? What would you say to this man?"

"Okay, I don't need to do this."

"Yes, you do. Pastor Jake, you need to say this so you can hear your own words."

Jake sighed. "I would tell him to trust Reggie Bennett. I would tell him to trust in God. I would pray with him that God would calm his fears and protect his wife. That's what I'd tell that man."

"You are that man. As your pastor, I'm telling you to trust God and to trust Reggie. Will you let me pray for you?" Jake nodded so Walt reached out and rested a hand on Jake's arm and began to pray for Jake. Even so, a tumult of emotion shook Jake, making him continue to doubt.

CHAPTER 31

With the creature dead, Sam was determined to not let Johnny or Sarah die now. He tried to find his way back to familiar territory, although he thought he was lost a few times. Sam knew that it was getting late. It had been a long time since he ate the pizza in his old house. If he didn't find something familiar soon, he'd be lost in the woods overnight. Gnats swarmed around his head as he kept on trudging through the thick foliage. He stopped when he saw broken sticks and torn leaves on a bush on his right. Leaning down, Sam saw the dried blood on a few of the leaves. He was headed in the right direction now.

With renewed energy, Sam pushed past the bush and followed the splatters of blood to a familiar place in the woods. It took longer than he thought it would, but Sam finally made it back to the rocks where the caves were. He ran into the dark cave and stopped, waiting for his eyes to adjust to the dark interior.

"Johnny, I'm back," Sam said. He heard Johnny moving around in the cage.

"Hey, thought you forgot us," Johnny replied from the darkness. "What took you so long?"

"I ran into Trevor and the creature in the woods."

"Where are they?" Sam could hear the fear in Johnny's voice.

"I don't know where Trevor is. But the creature was shot."

"Shot! Is he alive?" Johnny asked. "Was anyone else hurt?"

"The creature is dead. I don't know about anyone else. I ran away and got lost in the woods for a while."

"You've got to get us out of here. Can you go back to your old house?"

"Well, if the people who live there now are home, the police are probably there."

"Why?"

"I broke into the house this morning. I guess that doesn't matter now. Hang tight. I'll be back as soon as I can."

"Hey, last time you told me that, you were gone for hours," Johnny said sarcastically.

"I'll hurry," Sam said and quickly left.

Sam hurried through the woods. He was bothered as he realized that Sarah hadn't moved once. Even if Trevor had drugged her before he left the cave, that had been hours ago. Certainly by now, the drugs would had worn off. He practically ran through the woods toward the house.

Sam could see the lights at the house through the woods. There was no sign of police cars, but maybe the owner could go back with Sam to the caves. He ran into the backyard and to the kitchen door.

"Hey, I need some help in the woods," Sam called out, knocking.

"Who's out there?" a man's voice asked from inside.

"There's some people who need help in the woods. Can you help me?" Sam yelled.

A man came to door and looked out of the window at Sam. He was tall and thin with dark wavy hair. He opened the inside door. "Who are you?"

"My name is Sam. There are some people trapped in a cave in the woods."

"Do you know anything about my house getting broken into today?" He narrowed his eyes.

"Look, can you help me and then ask me questions?" Sam asked, stepping away from the door. He thought of the other houses on the street and started backing up.

"No, you don't!" The man opened the storm door and rushed Sam. "Suzie, call the cops," he shouted over his shoulder. Sam turned to run and the man grabbed him from behind. Sam struggled, but the man was strong and kept yelling to his wife to call the cops. He pushed Sam onto the ground and his wife came running out with the cordless phone.

"Marv," she yelled. "What are you doing?"

"This is the kid who broke into our house today. Did you get the cops?" He twisted Sam's arm behind him.

"Listen to me," Sam said gasping. "Yes, I broke in earlier. But there are two people trapped in a cave in the woods...."

"Nice try, kid. We'll wait for the cops to straighten this out." Marv hauled Sam to his feet. He took Sam to a tool shed next to his new two car garage. "Suzie, open the shed."

"You can't put him in there," she said, following her husband.

"Sure, I can. He can't get away from in there."

"Please, don't do this. There are two people who need help...." Sam tried to explain again.

Suzie opened the shed and Marv pushed him inside. He closed it and then used a padlock to lock Sam in. Sam pounded on the inside of the shed, yelling.

With no windows, it was pitch dark, and Sam was being poked in the back by some garden tools.

"Just cool off, kid. I'm sure the cops won't take long to get here," Marv said, his voice fading away as he went back to the house.

In frustration, Sam grabbed the shovel that was poking him and began slamming on the inside of the shed door.

"Hey," Marv yelled. "You break anything in there and you'll just get yourself in more trouble."

"We need to get back to the people. Mrs. Peterson needs medical help!" Sam yelled. He put his ear against the door. Hearing nothing, he yelled again. "Listen to me, if she dies, it'll be your fault!"

Sam started banging on the door again with the shovel. He turned and started hitting other stuff in the shed. He had no idea what he was hitting, but it was causing a lot of noise.

"Stop it!" Marv said coming back to the shed. "If you break anything, I'll kill you!"

Sam didn't stop even though he could hear Marv yelling. He wouldn't stop until Marv opened the door and he could get back to the woods. Sam knocked over glass jars full of nails, nuts, and bolts. The crash was deafening, and Sam could hear glass and hardware falling all over the small shed.

"That's it!" Marv just about screamed. "You break into my house and now you destroy my shed." Marv fumbled with the lock and yanked the door opened. Sam pushed against the door as soon as he heard Marv begin to open it. Sam threw Marv off balance and he stumbled backwards.

The element of surprise caught Marv off guard and the shock of his destroyed glass jars, ruined tools, and broken frame on his daughter's bike caused him to hesitate for just a few seconds, long enough for Sam to take off for the woods. Sam heard Marv swearing and yelling behind him. But Sam had the advantage in the woods, he knew it from his years of playing there as a child. He just hoped Marv would tell the police that he was headed for the caves.

CHAPTER 32

Meg sat on the hard vinyl chairs in the waiting room outside the operating room. Rachel had joined Meg at the hospital about a half an hour after she got there. The two cried and consoled each other while waiting for news. Then Meg called Michael to tell him about their father. She was shocked when her mother walked in with him.

Meg hugged her mother and Michael. She held her breath when her mother saw Rachel. The two acknowledged each other, and then her mother sat on the far side of the waiting room. It had been hours since Michael and her mother arrived at the hospital, and there was no further information about her father.

Afternoon had long since passed and her mother began to complain about being hungry. Meg refused to leave, and her attitude bothered Michael. Rachel watched the whole exchange and then walked over to them.

"Sylvia, I'll go with you to the cafeteria if you'd like," Rachel said. "I'm getting hungry, too."

Sylvia looked at her children and rose. "Sure you don't want to join us?" she said in a tight voice, glaring at Michael.

He looked at Meg, then shook his head. "That's okay. You go ahead."

Sylvia sighed and left with Rachel. Meg watched the two women leave and raised her eyebrows at Michael. "Mom's going to kill you later," Meg said.

"What do you mean?" he asked.

"Mom's question was more like a command. You know...'come with me, Michael.' You didn't catch that?"

"No, she can take of herself. I'm more worried about you than Mom."

"Why are you worried about me?" Meg was surprised.

"I just see something in your eyes...."

"Just stop, Michael. I don't need you to play counselor to me." Michael sighed and sat back with a disgusted look on his face. "What now?" continued Meg. "Mad at me, real mature, Mickey."

"Not mad, worried about you."

"Well, stop worrying."

"Why should I? Next time, you won't be so lucky. The bad guy won't be the one that ends up dead."

Meg stood up and walked to a vending machine. She put her hands on the top of the machine and looked interested in the candy bars and snacks, but then looked back to see Michael watching her. They were alone in the waiting room.

"You don't think that I'm aware that Dad could be the one dead? If Jake wasn't there, he would be." Meg's voice was shaking.

"Dad only got involved to protect you. And if he lives, he'll probably lose his job once Bennett realizes how deeply involved he was into the investigation."

Meg turned and sank down in a chair next the machines. "Stop. I know all this."

"Do you really understand?"

"Yes, Dad and I had a long talk yesterday. We talked about the past and everything finally felt okay between us. I even felt safe last night for the first time since I found out Grant escaped. And it was because Dad was with me."

"I'm glad you finally talked to him. Real timely too...you know..." Michael stammered not knowing how to finish his sentence.

"He's not going to die," Meg whispered fiercely. "He can't, not now."

They fell into silence, each lost in thought. Finally Meg said, "I thought you were going to try and make me feel better, not worse."

"Sorry, this just sucks."

"Yeah, I know. Is this how you work with people in therapy?"

"No, not really. You're my sister so it's different talking to you. You always have to have your own way." He smirked.

"Hey, what did I do to you?"

"Aside from tormenting me my whole life?"

"That's only cause you're a spoiled brat," Meg said, returning the smirk. "I hate all this waiting and not knowing what's happening."

"Mmm, major control issues. I don't think there's any chance of recovery for you."

Meg stuck her tongue out at Michael, and he laughed at her. Meg crossed her arms and sank down in the chair. Michael sighed and shifted in his seat. "Can I ask you something else?"

"More therapy? Are you sure I'm ready for this, doctor?"

"Seriously," he asked. Meg shrugged. "What happens now to Jake?"

"I don't know. Last I saw him, Bennett had someone drive him home."

"Are you just going to drop this now that you got what you wanted? Are you forgetting about Sarah?"

"I'm sure that Bennett is looking for her. They will back track Trevor's moves...."

"And if they can't find her? Are you going to get back involved to help Jake find her?"

"What can I do? Bennett isn't going to let me help."

"Bennett didn't want you to help in the first place. Now you're going to just walk away. There's got to be something you can do, something you figured out."

"I'm going to talk to Bennett and give him all the information we have. But we really didn't figure out where Grant was. It really was a coincidence that we ran into him in the woods."

"Okay, but what about Jake? He got involved because he wanted you to help him find his wife. She hasn't been found. Are you just going to drop this now when Jake probably needs you more than ever?"

"Michael, when Jake realized Trevor was dead, he just lost it. Bennett had to pull him off the body. It was like he was a broken man. To be honest, I think it finished him. Everything he's done, everything he says, it's all about her. The way he looks when he talks about her. The driving force behind him working on the investigation was just to find Sarah."

"Are you okay?"

"What do you mean?"

"Do you still love Jake? You moved out of Granelle because he got engaged."

"No, I'm not still in love with Jake. I haven't really talked to him in years. He's not the same man I was in love with. He's too religious for me."

"Can you live with that?" Michael was pressuring her.

"I happen to have a life without Jake, you know," Meg said, looking at Michael. "I do hope that they find Sarah for Jake's sake. Sometimes when I tell a wife her husband has been cheating on her, she gets that same destroyed look that Jake had today. Makes me feel really bad for that person. I don't want Jake to feel that way, because he's still my friend. Nothing else."

"Are you sure?" Michael asked again.

"Yes, I was in love with a fantasy that I had about what my life would be like with Jake. But I wasn't in love with Jake. I guess it's time for me to remember that I was the one that broke up with him, not the other way around."

"Good." Michael smiled at her. "I'm glad you finally realized that."

"I do have a life outside of Granelle. I have a great business and make good money. A few weeks ago, I started seeing a Saratoga city cop. He's name is Kurt and he's really cute."

"Oh?"

"I'm not rushing anything. But I do enjoy spending time with him and talking to him. He's probably wondering what's happened to me the past few days."

Michael looked at his watch and changed the subject. "Do you think that the surgery is taking too long?"

Meg sobered for a minute. "He should be out by now. I hope everything is okay."

Rachel and Sylvia came in, talking like old friends. They sat down together near Michael. Meg and Michael exchanged a look of surprise.

"What's up with you two?" Meg asked.

They both looked at Meg and then each other. Sylvia looked back at Meg, "You know, sometimes it's nice to just move on. We happen to have a lot in common."

Meg continued to just stare at them. Michael joined their conversation and Meg decided to find out why the surgery was taking so long.

CHAPTER 33

Dark shadows filled the woods as Sam raced back toward the caves. Night was beginning to fall, and he hoped that they would be able to get Mrs. Peterson to safety before it was too dark. He just hoped Marv was mad enough to get the police to follow Sam into the woods. As he got close to the caves, he thought he heard sirens in the distance.

Sam stepped inside the cave and realized dusk was falling. "Hey," he called out.

"What took you so long? I thought you said you were coming right back... with help!" Johnny said.

"Well, the new owners of my old house weren't too happy to see me. The guy threw me into his shed for a while." Sam slid up to the cage.

"Did you tell him about us?"

"I tried to, but he was more interested in locking me up and calling the police. Hopefully he heard me say I was headed up here."

"What if he doesn't? What if no one comes?"

"I'll have to go back out to Dunning Road and try a different neighbor. But I thought I heard sirens when I got back here."

"Sam," Johnny said a little hesitantly. "It's almost dark. What if Trevor comes back?"

Sam didn't say anything. He thought about the creature again and sadness washed over him. "Sam?" Johnny said into the dark cave. He couldn't see Sam's face. "What are we going to do?"

"If Trevor was going to come back, he probably would have by now. It's been hours since I saw him."

"But what if he does?" Johnny asked with fear in his voice.

"I don't know, Johnny. Don't panic."

"I'm scared and just want to get out of here. Mrs. Peterson hasn't been awake all day today. She's getting pretty sick."

"I'm sure you'll be out soon. Let me head back toward Dunning and see if the police are at my old house."

"Maybe you should try a different house."

"Why?"

"Because if that guy called the cops on you, they won't wait for you to explain until you're at the police station. I don't think Mrs. Peterson can wait much longer to see a doctor."

"Oh, okay." Sam got up and headed toward the cave entrance.

"Hey, Sam, get back quick. I just want to get out of here."

Sam headed out of the cave. The sky had turned a dark blue and the stars were coming out. The heat of the day was still in the air and Sam crept back to the old path that led to Dunning Road. So far, he could see no one headed toward the caves. With the darkness in the woods, Sam headed back to the house out of instinct rather than sight.

The police cruiser was in the driveway, but everyone was in the house. Sam thought about what Johnny had said, but this was the quickest way to get help. He stood at the edge of the woods and yelled. No one responded.

Sam yelled again. "Can anyone hear me?"

A door slammed, and Sam could tell someone came out of the kitchen door and stood looking toward the woods. Since the light was on the person's back, Sam couldn't tell who it was.

"Hey," Sam yelled again. "There's some people locked up in a cage in the woods. They need help."

"Who's out there?" the person yelled.

"This is Sam. Who are you?"

"This is Officer Matthews. You need to come down here and explain yourself."

"No, you need to just follow me into the woods. Mrs. Peterson is there and she's sick."

"This is not a time to play games, Sam. Now get over here where I can see you," Officer Matthews demanded.

"Just call Captain Bennett. I want to talk to a cop that knows what he's doing. I'm sure he won't waste time getting to the caves to help Mrs. Peterson."

Officer Matthews swore at Sam and headed toward the woods. Sam heard a noise to his left. He quickly turned and ran deeper into the woods. He heard cursing behind him as Marv ran into branches. Sam moved further away and ducked behind a large pine tree. He could see Marv fumbling around in the woods as the officer got a flashlight out and joined the search for Sam.

Crouching low, Sam quietly cut over toward the backyard of another neighbor. There weren't too many houses on this street, but he did remember a Mrs.

Claiborne who had lived at the next house down on Dunning on the other side of a thick grove. He glanced back and saw that Marv and Officer Matthews had found the path and were following it. It didn't directly lead to the caves, so Sam doubted they would find Johnny.

It took him another five minutes to push his way through the thick woods to the Claiborne's backyard. He saw a dim light on in an upstairs window. Sam skirted around the house and got to the front door. There was no doorbell, so Sam pounded on the door and called out. A light came on downstairs and then the porch light flicked on.

"Who's there?" an elderly voice called out.

"Mrs. Claiborne, this is Sam Craig. We used to be neighbors," Sam said through the door.

"The Craigs moved and don't live next door anymore," she replied through the door.

"We moved to Poughkeepsie. But I've been visiting my friend in town the past few weeks. I need you to call the police station and ask Captain Bennett to come here. I have to talk to him."

"Why don't you just call yourself? Don't all you kids have cell phones now?"

"I don't have my phone. Can you please just call? I'll wait on the porch here if you're afraid to have me come in."

"That's probably best. I'll call, you wait there."

Sam sighed as he sat on the porch. Another delay. He waited for a few minutes. Mosquitoes buzzed around him and he batted a few away. The porch light was drawing all kinds of bugs out. Finally she came back, "You still out there, boy?"

"Yes, ma'am."

"I was told to tell you to wait here. There's an officer next door who will come talk to you."

"I already tried talking to him. He won't listen to me. There's two people trapped in the woods. I need to get them help. Can you please call back and ask Captain Bennett to come out?"

"I already told you what they said."

Sam looked down the road. It was another long walk to the only other house that had people living in it. At this rate, he should just go back to the Hanson house and call from his cell phone. Sam got off the porch and headed down the dark road. He hated the thought of going back to that house now, in the dark, alone. But he had to get help. He heard a car coming and glanced back to Mrs. Claiborne's house. He saw the police cruiser pull in and crouched behind some bushes. After a few moments, he decided to go to the next house. Sam followed the road from just inside the woods in case the cruiser decided to check out the road.

The other neighbor's house was also deep in the woods. The driveway was long and Sam couldn't even see lights on. But he turned up the driveway, hoping that someone was there.

A car pulled in, washing Sam in light. He ducked into the woods. The car pulled up to where Sam ducked in. The window came down and Sam strained to see who was in the car.

"Sam, just come out. I saw you go into the trees," Reggie's voice boomed out. Sam stood quietly waiting. "Don't make this more difficult on yourself. You have some things to answer for. Let's go to the station and talk about this."

"No," Sam said, still hiding behind a tree. "I found Mrs. Peterson and Johnny in the woods and no one will listen to me."

Reggie's voice got angry, "That's not something to joke about."

"I'm not joking! If you take me to the station, it will just waste a lot of time. Mrs. Peterson is sick and needs a doctor now!"

Reggie opened the door and got out. Sam backed away and Reggie heard the sound. "Don't take off on me, Sam. If what you say is true, I don't want to have to look for you."

"It feels like I left them hours ago."

"Let me just call for backup...." Reggie said reaching in the car.

"No!" Sam yelled. "You just want to trick me."

"Tell me, what have you done to show me I can trust what you're saying?"

"Nothing. But I can't get them out alone or I would have already."

"Since you don't trust me and I don't trust you, what now?"

"Just come with me into the woods. You'll know soon enough if I'm lying. If I'm not, you'll be there to help me get them out."

"Is Johnny sick too?"

"Not that I can tell."

"Then why didn't he just come with you?"

"They are locked in a cage. Like the one that I was in the last time. Johnny said that Trevor took the key with him and there was nothing there to break the lock with."

"Okay, I'll go with you. Let me get a flashlight and some tools from my trunk. But if you're lying to me, Sam, I will have you before a family court judge tomorrow morning. Do I make myself clear?"

"Just hurry up so she doesn't die."

Sam waited inside the trees for Reggie, who grunted as he walked up to Sam. Sam took the lead, directing Reggie through the thick woods. They skirted through the side lawn of the dark house and reentered the woods in back of the house. The night had fallen and it was pitch black. Clouds covered any light from the moon. Branches grabbed at their clothes and mosquitoes buzzed around them.

Reggie recognized the cave area when they got closer. He reached out and stopped Sam. "This area was already explored. No one was here."

"They're here now. Come on, it can't hurt you to just look in the one cave with me." Sam jerked away from Reggie. He ran on ahead and ducked into the cave. Reggie sighed and followed, feeling disappointed that this was just another one of Sam's games.

As Reggie stepped into the cave, he heard Sam talking to someone. He shone the flashlight around and saw Sam on his knees next to Johnny in the cage. Reggie was shocked to see the cage and rushed up to it. When he saw Sarah, he grabbed the lock and pulled at it. After working on the lock, Reggie finally broke it and opened the cage. He rushed to Sarah and checked her vitals.

Reggie pulled a cell phone out of his pocket and called for an ambulance to meet them at Marv's while Johnny got out of the cage and went outside with Sam.

"I didn't think you were ever going to get anyone to come back with you," Johnny said, breathing in the night air.

"It's been a long time since anyone actually listened to me. Took a while to convince Captain Bennett I wasn't lying once he finally showed up."

"Sam, Johnny," Reggie called out. "I need your help in here." The boys went back into the cave. Reggie was picking up Sarah. "I'm going to have to carry her out of the woods. Sam, since you know the woods the best, you lead us with the flashlight. Johnny, I need you to help push the trees back so that they don't hit Mrs. Peterson in her face. Okay? Let's move."

It took longer to get back to the house with Reggie carrying Sarah. Although she was small, she was dead weight. Her shallow breathing concerned Reggie, so he pushed himself to move as fast as he could. Finally, they walked out the woods into a fully lit backyard. The paramedics were waiting and Reggie gently laid Sarah down on a stretcher.

Marv glared at Sam while Greg Matthews tried to avoid his boss, knowing he had messed up again. Sam glanced around the yard and saw a news van pulling up in back of the police cruiser. He tapped Reggie's arm and pointed.

Reggie nodded and led Sam and Johnny to an unmarked police car. He told another officer to drive the boys to the Mendoza house and told Sam to stay put for now.

CHAPTER 34

With a feeling of dread, Jake opened the door for Reggie. He was certain it was bad news. To his surprise, Reggie said, "Sarah has been found. I'm here to drive you to the hospital."

"What?"

"I'll explain on the way. Come on."

Jake quickly followed Reggie out to the police cruiser. As Reggie pulled out of the driveway, he put on the siren and raced toward Saratoga Hospital.

"Where was she found?" Jake asked as soon as they were on the road.

"In those caves behind Dunning Road," Reggie said, glancing at Jake.

"How is she?"

"Don't know yet. She was unconscious when I got to her."

"Like those women before," Jake said softly. "I didn't think Grant had her in town. What made you think to look in the caves again?"

"It was the Craig boy. He found her with Johnny locked in a cage."

"Sam Craig?"

"Took him quite a bit of time to get help. I finally decided to go out and see what was going on after two people on Dunning Road called about a kid causing trouble. Matthews was out there and just wasn't handling it very well. Sam had broken into a house earlier today and Matthews was too busy trying to bust him for breaking and entering rather than listen to his story. I finally found him up the road and he convinced me to go with him."

"I thought he was somehow involved in Sarah's disappearance."

"Who? Sam?"

"Yes, that's what we thought."

"Where would you get that idea? It would make more sense for you to think Angelos did it." Jake didn't say anything; he just looked out the window. He didn't want to get into this with Reggie right now. But Reggie pressed him. "We've got a twenty minute drive, Jake. You might as well come clean with me. I'd rather hear your side first."

Jake looked over at his old friend and saw how angry he was. Yet Reggie was the one who was here, racing him to Sarah. Just like Pastor Walt, the two friends whom Jake had let down were the two friends to come to his rescue.

"I was going to talk to you this morning," Jake began. "I was convinced that I needed to tell you that Meg and I were investigating on our own. I was going to tell you everything I knew. Meg and Brian showed up last night saying that the boys were missing. We were going to help look for them. But when we found Sam's car at the Hanson place, we assumed he was involved. We were looking for him when we ran into Grant in the woods."

"Why didn't you call me when you found the car?"

"I know we acted impulsively. And I was concerned about telling you that Mr. Riley was involved. I didn't want to get him in trouble for trying to help us."

"What? I don't understand why you didn't trust me. I was your boss, and more than that, I'm your friend. I told you I was handling Sarah's case personally. Why did you go behind my back?"

"Grant called me. He told me if I got you involved he would kill Sarah. I was afraid for her life."

"And you didn't think I had enough experience to know how to handle a hostage situation? So you had to do it yourself? What did he want from you?"

"Sam," Jake said. The silence between them was long. As they came into the city limits, the road turned into a paved street, and street lights illuminated their drive. The hospital would be coming up soon.

Finally Reggie said, "You never should have gotten involved. You know it, too. I'll need a formal statement from you about everything that happened."

Jake nodded and didn't reply. He felt choked up as he looked at the ambulance bay. Sarah and Brian were in that hospital fighting for their lives. Jake hoped it wasn't too late for either one of them.

Meg sat next to her stepmother. Michael and Sylvia had left over an hour ago, just before a nurse came in to say there had been complications in the surgery. They had been sitting in silence ever since. Rachel wiped at tears that flowed down her cheeks, while Meg sat feeling guilty for allowing her father to be involved.

"Mrs. Riley," a nurse said from the doorway. Both women looked up. "Your husband is in recovery now. You can see him for a few minutes."

"How is he?" Meg asked, getting up.

"He's in critical condition. He suffered a heart attack during surgery. There was a lot of damage to his neck and shoulder, too. We will be keeping him in recovery overnight. Mrs. Riley, if you'll come with me, I'll take you to him."

Meg was left standing alone while Rachel hurried after the nurse. She sat back down in her seat, figuring she'd wait and find out how he was when Rachel returned. Meg thought about the past few days with her father, how he stood by her, risked his job and life, to be sure she had the help she needed. Now that they were reconnected, Meg didn't want to lose him this way.

Meg heard someone coming in and looked up to see Reggie. He came over and squeezed into a chair next to her.

"They never make these chairs big enough," Reggie grumbled. "How's your father?"

"Not too good. He's out of surgery, but he had a heart attack."

"Sorry to hear that. How you holding up?"

Meg just shook her head. "I can't lose him now."

"He's pretty tough. Gonna take more than this to stop him." Meg just looked down at the floor. She felt like crying, but fought it. Reggie went on, "Jake's down in the ER. Sarah was found."

"What a relief," she said. "How is she?"

"She's stable now. It's going to be a long recovery for her."

"Where did you find her?"

"She was in the caves. It was actually Sam Craig that found her."

"Sam...that's ironic."

"How so?" Reggie asked.

"We were looking for Sam."

Reggie scowled thinking about what Jake had told him. He didn't like the sound of that. "Why were you looking for Sam?"

Meg shrugged. "Doesn't matter now."

Reggie sat thinking for a few moments. "You were looking for Sam for Grant, weren't you?"

"No, I never would have given Sam to Grant. We just weren't thinking straight about anything."

"The very reason why none of you should have gotten involved in the first place."

Meg didn't answer him. Now, she wished he would just leave. "Look, Captain. I don't know what to tell you. If you want to blame someone for our involvement, blame me. I dragged Jake into this because of Sarah, and my father got involved to protect me. I was afraid and just wanted to find Grant before he found me."

"There's plenty of blame to go around."

"So did you come here to arrest me?" Meg looked over at Reggie.

"Not yet," he said, meeting her gaze.

"I didn't mean to kill Grant," Meg slouched down in the chair. She looked down at her hands. "It's just that creature was attacking Dad. I shot at that animal and Grant jumped in between. If Jake wasn't there, Dad would have been torn apart." When Reggie didn't say anything she asked, "What are you going to do now?"

"Don't know yet. I'll need to get statements from each of you first and then we'll go from there. At least this is finally over. With Grant dead, we won't have to worry about women missing in Granelle again."

"Thanks, Captain."

"For what?" he said, trying to get up from the chair.

"For being decent about this. I know I'm not your favorite person."

"Don't thank me yet. There's a real chance your father will be suspended and you could lose your P.I. license. But you probably knew the risks when you decided to undermine my investigation. Then, if the DA decides to pursue any criminal charges...." Reggie shrugged.

"Yeah, we knew the risks. But like I said, I was scared, and Dad was trying to protect me from myself. And Jake...."

"After I finish my reports, I'll talk to the D.A. I'm sure that given the circumstances and Grant's criminal record...but can't promise you anything. I'm going to go down and check with Jake. Sometime tomorrow, come to the station and give me your statement."

"Okay, as long as I don't have to talk to Matthews," Meg said with a smirk.

"No, you'll just have to deal with me."

Jake sat next to Sarah's bedside, holding her hand. Pastor Walt knocked on the door and Jake looked up. "Hey, how'd you know I was here?" Jake asked with a weary smile.

"Reggie Bennett again," Walt said coming to the bedside. He laid a hand on Jake's shoulder. "How is she?"

"Doctor says that she's severely dehydrated and showing signs of starvation. But he thinks with bed rest and time, she'll be okay. She's really strong."

"And the baby?" Walt asked gently.

"They found a heartbeat. But it's too early to tell. Doc says we'll have to keep an eye on her pregnancy."

"Well, I believe in miracles. I have a whole church full of folks praying for her."

"Thanks. She needs it."

"Can you take a break? I'd like to talk to you for a few minutes. Millie's here and she can sit with Sarah for a bit."

"Sure." Jake leaned over and kissed Sarah's cheek. Millie stood in the doorway. Jake walked over and hugged her. She sat down in Jake's chair and patted Sarah's arm. Once they were in the hall, the men walked quietly down a hall toward the elevators.

"I heard Mr. Riley's out of surgery," Walt began.

"If we hadn't goe into the woods, he wouldn't have needed surgery." Jake stopped walking. He leaned against the wall and sighed. "I should have stopped them from going."

"They wouldn't have listened to you. If you hadn't been there, he would be dead," Walt said putting his hand on Jake's shoulder. "You made some mistakes. But in the end, you were right where God needed you to be. Do you think Meg could have lived with herself if her father had been killed?"

"Probably not. I feel so guilty about what I did, the mistakes I made."

"That's because you still need to talk this out with Reggie. You betrayed his trust and friendship. I'm sure by now, he knows about everyone's involvement. But you need to be honest with him and repair your friendship with him."

"Reggie's not the only one, though," Jake said, looking at his old friend. "I'm sorry that I didn't come to you sooner. And how do I explain my actions to the church board?"

"In the same way. Be honest about what you did. Jake, we know you are human and that you love your wife. Sometimes it's hard being in a leadership position and admit that you were wrong and made mistakes. But in those mistakes, you'll grow. You won't take lightly your relationship with Sarah again."

"That's for sure. I want to be there when she opens her eyes and tell her how much I love her."

"And you should be."

"What about the church?"

"The church isn't going anywhere. You've got some things to tend to first. When you're ready and Sarah's back on her feet, you and I will talk again."

"Are the elders going to trust me to run the church again?"

"I'm sure some will question your judgment. But for now, the elders are leaving that decision to me. Like I said, take some time. Spend some time with the Lord and when you're ready, we will talk about getting you back. I'm too old to run the church for long, you know," Walt said with a smile. "Now, you go back to Sarah. Millie doesn't like me to be up this late anymore. She made an exception for you tonight."

The two men headed back toward the emergency room. As they stepped into the room, Millie stood and hugged Jake before leaving with Walt. As Jake sat back in the chair and took her hand, Sarah opened her eyes and smiled at him.

CHAPTER 35

Sam and Johnny sat on the front porch. Sam's duffel bag was in his car and he was ready to leave for home. He finally talked to his father this morning about all that had happened in the past week. Stanley was taking a flight out that night and would be back in Poughkeepsie tomorrow. For Sam, it was too little too late.

"Dad said to tell you the offer is still open if you want to come back and stay with us," Johnny said.

"Depends on what happens with my father and Anne now. As long as your father has no plans on forcing me to finish high school, I might consider it." Sam stretched his legs out in front of him.

"I told him about your school problems. Our school has a GED program that you might be able to get into."

"I'll keep that in mind," Sam said, standing up. "Guess I'd better head on home."

Johnny stood and they walked over to Sam's car. They said a few awkward good-byes and finally Sam pulled out of the driveway.

The drive back to Poughkeepsie was uneventful. He was glad his father hadn't been able to get a flight back from his honeymoon until tomorrow. This would give Sam one night to have the house to himself without a bunch of questions. As Sam pulled the car into the driveway, he looked up at the big white house that never felt like home. He was relieved to be here now. Sam climbed out and took his duffel bag out of the backseat. He walked to the back of the house and unlocked the door.

As Sam walked in, he felt for the first time like this was really home. The past few weeks, being in Granelle, had helped him realize that Poughkeepsie had become his home a long time ago. He dropped his duffel bag by the door and went into the kitchen for some soda. The message light on the phone was blinking and he pushed the play button. He listened as he poured a glass of soda and noticed the pile of mail by the front door. Anne had insisted that they get a mail slot, so that the mail could always be dropped inside and no one would know if the mail hadn't been picked up.

Sam went to the door and began picking up the stack of mail that had accumulated over the past few weeks. He picked up a fat envelope with strange stamps on it and was surprised to see it was for him. Setting the pile of mail on a small table by the door, Sam opened the envelope. Inside were a typewritten letter from an attorney in Ireland and a handwritten letter. The attorney introduced himself as representing the estate of Shamus O'Leary and urged Sam's legal guardian to contact him upon receipt of the letter. Sam quickly dismissed the letter and began to read the other one.

> Dear Sam,
>
> If you have received this letter, I have died. You probably have heard of me by now. I am Shamus O'Leary, the last keeper. Trevor was to have been the keeper after me, but the creature refused to accept him in my place. Instead, he chose you.
>
> I failed in the end. In fear, I left the creature behind and did not properly prepare you to take over as the new keeper. But the power that the creatures possess is strong, and you will not be left ill-prepared to carry out your responsibilities. In fact, I was able to carry out the ritual necessary to make you the new keeper prior to my death with the help of my old friend and attorney, Donovan. Over the next few years at various intervals, you will receive letters from me explaining everything.
>
> Upon your eighteenth birthday, you will be bequeathed my entire fortune. This is not for you to spend in a frivolous manner, but for you to use in carrying on the long tradition. This inheritance has been passed down from keeper to keeper. You will need to find a lawyer that you can trust. Donovan will help you.
>
> Should you fail to protect the creature, you will be punished. I know you met him. His mate died while under my care and he will have found another. It is your responsibility to protect him and any offspring he may have by humans.
>
> I must warn you that there is a man who can harm you. You know him as Pastor Jake. He is dangerous to you because he is a man of prayer. Even though there is much power in being the keeper, the power that is in prayer is greater. This is one lesson that Trevor refused to accept and believe. In the end, it was his undoing. Don't allow anyone who prays get close to you.

Do not let anyone know of these things. Donovan will try to tell your father, to warn him of danger. But the danger you face will come from failure to protect the creatures. You were chosen. This is your destiny.

Shamus

Sam read the letter twice before carefully folding it up. He thought of the creature dying in Granelle. But instinctively, he knew to bury him before he was found by the police. Sam worried that he had already failed. He went back to the door and grabbed his duffel bag. He went up the stairs to his room to hide the letters from his father.

Sam had a spot under his bed where there were a few loose boards in the floor. He went through his duffel bag to find the satchel with the old journals in it. Pushing his bed from the wall, Sam knelt down and pried the loose boards up. He took out some old treasures he had hidden in there before and stuck the letters and the satchel in the hole. He put the boards back, looked around his room, and grabbed a few old magazines, tossing them on the spot. Then he pushed the bed back in place.

Sam went to the bedroom window and looked out at the woods behind his house. He found the spot where he had seen the red eyes so many times and stood staring. Sam suddenly realized that some nights, there were more than one set of eyes. Out there in the woods, there were others.

Sam turned and ran out of the house. He went into the woods and searched around on the ground near the trees. He saw the trampled grass and the large footprints. He looked around and then took off into the woods, led by instinct. Sam walked further in, pushing through tangled undergrowth. Finally, in a small clearing, Sam found them. One of them stood when Sam came into view. Sam collapsed to his knees and the creatures stared at him.

Sam finally said, "I'm sorry. He followed me to Granelle. I didn't know...I didn't know that I was supposed to protect him." Tears filled Sam's eyes and his vision blurred. He dropped his head to his hands. "I'm sorry, I didn't know." Sam felt hot breath on his hands and dropped them. The male stood before him. There was a knowing in the creature's eyes. "You understand me just like your father did," Sam said.

The creature put his paw on Sam's knee and sat down. He looked past the male to the smaller female who sat away from them. She growled at Sam as he reached out and stroked the other creature's large head. "It's not safe for you here. There aren't enough woods. But I know a place where there are a lot of woods away from people. You will be safe until I'm eighteen and can come to take care of you. I'll take you up there right now. No one will know. It's a little town up in the mountains. It's called Granelle."

About the Author

Ladean Warner received her MBA from Empire State College and is currently working on her doctorate in Business Administration at Walden University. Ladean works as a finance director for a girls' school. In addition, she is a motivational speaker and professional life coach.

Ladean lives in upstate New York and enjoys spending time with her husband, three children, and grandson. She is involved in her local church, is an avid reader, and enjoys other creative pursuits. Ladean's writing brings together her love of suspense stories and her deep faith in God.

Ladean offers her special thanks to her dear friends, Liz Marcuccio, Barbara Griffin, Jonnel Garrant, and Karie Garrow for all your help. She also wishes to thank her favorite photographer, Jami LaCasse, for providing a a great photo for the cover.

Ladean's first novel, *The Keeper of Darkness*, is available at www.ladeanwarner.com.